MW01138733

More Than Meets the Eye

Melissa Finger

TRILOGY CHRISTIAN PUBLISHERS

TUSTIN, CA

Trilogy Christian Publishers
A Wholly Owned Subsidary of Trinity Broadcasting Network
2442 Michelle Drive
Tustin, CA 92780

Cover design by: Jeff Summers

For information about special discounts for bulk purchases, please contact Trilogy Christian Publishing.

Manufactured in the United States of America

10 9 8 7 6 5 4 3 2 1

Library of Congress Cataloging-in-Publication Data is available.

ISBN: 978-1-63769-814-3

E-ISBN: 978-1-63769-815-0

Contents

Dedication

This book is dedicated to survivors of trauma. While this book is fiction, I hope it will honor the struggle and the many challenges that trauma survivors face every day. Sudden shifts in perspective, lost time, and spiritual battles are a reality for these individuals. If you feel a little lost or confused at moments, just know that it's a fairly accurate reflection of how these survivors live life. Their courage and bravery to get up and face the world each day is amazing and a gift from God.

If I were to assign a purpose to this book, it would be to stretch your imagination about how or why God allows things to happen. It would be to encourage you to think beyond our lives here on earth and to think about the kingdom of heaven and eternity. While God deeply cares about all of our pain and sorrow here, He also calls us to fight a spiritual battle alongside Him. He will win, and when we can align with His perspective, even for a moment, we will be able to see we have far more victories than we do defeats.

Chapter 1

Ronan stood in the shadow of a tall, cherry wood bookcase. His angelic stature was tall and strong. Gentle waves of brown hair barely touched the top of his broad shoulders. He nodded in approval as his green eyes passed over the room. The air was thick, though the room was well-lit. Ronan could sense the presence of the Lord resting in the small office.

His charge, Mary, was sitting in an oversized beige chair, going through her notes to prepare for her next client.

Suddenly, a dark shadow darted through the room but met its demise at the end of a sword that came out of nowhere. Ronan gave a slight nod of approval toward the warrior who had made the move. The soldier returned the nod and stepped back into his position beside Mary's large picture window.

Mary was a small-town therapist in her fifties. She had a gentle appearance. Her long-time experience of warring against evil could not be seen on her face.

Gentle wrinkles graced her eyes when she smiled. Her hair was beginning to show her age. It was pulled back in a bun on top of her head, with her glasses propped against it. Mary continued to flip casually through the pages of her notebook. If she was able to sense the thickness in the air, one couldn't tell by looking.

As Ronan looked around the room, two more black balls darted in. With one swoosh of a sword, they were gone.

"The warfare will be intense today," Ronan commented to Gabe, the newest warrior assigned to his group. "The storm has been building. The Most High God is preparing for a mighty victory!"

The enemy of God had also been preparing for this battle, and it would happen within the hour.

Gabe was wide-eyed as he looked around the room. "Are we prepared?"

"We are."

Gabe's stature was slightly smaller than Ronan's but still impressive. His manner indicated a meekness that was often carried by warriors new to the battle. His short hair and deep blue eyes gave him a youthful look, even though he had been a part of the army of God since the creation of the earth.

Ronan and Gabe, along with the others in this angelic army, were well aware of the dark cloud growing in size and strength several hundred yards above Mary's office.

Gabe motioned toward their charge. "What do you know of her?"

Ronan paused momentarily to listen to the sound of metal on metal high above the office. He knew demonic forces were already trying to enter the guarded space and engaging the army of the Lord.

"She is a powerful servant of the Most High God," he stated as he redirected his attention to Mary.

"In this place?"

Gabe looked around the unassuming office. A few decorative pieces hung on the walls displaying Scripture verses, nature scenes, or other inspirational designs. The room itself was small. There was just enough room for a desk, a large couch, two bookshelves, and, of course, Mary's oversized chair.

"I was surprised as well," Ronan continued. "Throughout time, I have been assigned to watch and defend people in powerful positions here on earth. When I was assigned to Mary, I was unsure as to why."

Gabe nodded in agreement.

"She rarely engaged in the type of battle that I had been fighting for centuries. Not even the type of client Mary worked with seemed like any of the charges I have had before." Ronan tilted his head as he reflected on his history with Mary. "Nonetheless, I took my post and faithfully served by her side through two different jobs and several office location changes. Then, about eight years ago, Mary started learning about severe trauma. She realized that she had a few clients who struggled with dissociation from childhood abuse."

"That still doesn't seem like a battle worthy of a warrior such as yourself," Gabe commented. "Shouldn't she have a great band of ministering angels assigned to bring comfort and understanding to her and her clients?"

As Gabe spoke, both warriors could sense the dark cloud over Mary's office expanding and slowly lowering toward the building. Ronan dispatched two additional warriors to the battle and then continued to speak.

"Somewhere in those eight years, Mary began to assist with Cindy's healing journey. When that day came, I understood why I had been sent to Mary."

"Cindy is her next client?"

Ronan nodded. "She is. Cindy's childhood was the worst of the worst. Her parents had chosen to give her over to darkness and evil at a young age. Cindy lived through decades of ritual abuse. It was only in her twenties when she was finally able to break free. She began seeing Mary in her thirties and had been working with her ever since."

"When I served in the heavenlies with the hosts of heaven, I heard stories of RA here on earth," Gabe paused as his thoughts drifted for a moment. "The enemy has a complex strategy in place," he continued.

"Indeed he does. I have seen a fair share of battles in this very office over the past four years, not just for Cindy but for many, many others." Ronan paused again as the battle outside gained intensity. "Today's battle preparation seems to be especially tense."

Mary had begun typing on her computer. Cindy would arrive in thirty minutes.

Gabe looked at the small woman casually typing notes and checking emails. He was beginning to understand the vast nature of Mary's work for the kingdom of God. "Is she ready?" he asked.

"By the looks of things, I would assume so."

Even the silence was heavy. A few dark spirits would occasionally make it through the guard outside and charge the space guarded by Ronan and the others. They each met their doom in an instant.

As the minutes passed, Ronan could feel his strength building. "She's praying," he stated matter-of-factly.

Gabe could feel it too. The power of prayer coursed through him. A subtle glow came from his sheathed sword.

"How can you tell the prayers are her's and not someone else's? She is still typing."

"I just know."

The sword fighting outside was getting closer and louder.

As Cindy arrived, Ronan and Gabe both felt a shift in the air around them. Gabe subconsciously let out a long breath he hadn't realized he was holding.

Mary greeted Cindy with a smile and offered her a bottle of water as they settled into the plush office chairs. The office was a cheery, pale yellow, and the furniture had been chosen for comfort. Despite the darkness preparing to invade the small office, the room felt like a peaceful spring day. This was normal for Mary and her work. The contrast between the spiritual and natural perspectives was vast, but it allowed clients to relax easier and feel at peace with the Lord. Ronan liked it, and he sensed the Lord took pleasure in it as well.

Darkness had begun to seep into the room as soon as Cindy entered, grasping for any last hold before the real battle began. As Mary prayed her usual opening prayer, the darkness held its position restrained by an invisible force field. The spiritual battle was just outside of the room now. Demons who entered with the dark cloud were forced to be still by the power of the Lord, and a special protection was given, which kept the darkness from touching Mary or Cindy, but the darkness was consuming every space behind the holy shield. Another shift happened around Ronan and Gabe. It was too dark now to tell what the shift was exactly, but the atmosphere in the room definitely shifted.

Cindy was sitting on the edge of the couch as she asked, "Did you get my emails?"

"I did. It appears it has been a difficult week. Is there any place, in particular, you would like to start?"

Cindy's face writhed with pain as she answered, "I'm not sure. I'm just so tired. I don't remember most of the week, but what I do remember is terrible." A few tears slipped down her cheeks. "I desperately need to find a new job, but I don't sleep well, and I am struggling just to keep myself together most days," she paused. "I'm not sure how much longer I can do this."

Mary nodded and made a few notes. "There is nothing easy about the journey you are taking," Mary paused as the words reached Cindy. Her body relaxed with the validation, but her face still showed her pain. "Let's begin in the courtroom of the Most High God, and we will see where we should start today."

Mary's warm smile was all the comfort Cindy could handle. She nodded and closed her eyes. As Mary began the courtroom prayer, the darkness in the room thickened. If Mary were not aware of what was happening before, she was now, but her prayer remained smooth and effortless.

Gabe was surprised by the level of warfare they were encountering. "Who is Cindy?" he asked with a deeper appreciation as to what her journey must have been.

"To answer that, we must go back a few years. Michael, would you like to answer?"

Michael was a towering figure who had walked in with Cindy and her spiritual entourage. His stature rivaled that of Ronan, and his stride was even and confident.

"Cindy has been my charge for many, many years," Michael began. "Her story is filled with great pain and sorrow.

"Each of her parents was a slave to evil in their own way from childhood. The tradition of evil and abuse of every kind went on for many generations, and unfortunately, they had given in to the evils around them. Cindy's mother never really wanted to be a part of that world, but her hope was gone, so she followed those who were leading her. Cindy's father was consumed with the lusts of greed and power that came with the darkness. He made choices that reinforced the evil in Cindy's bloodline."

Gabe could hear the compassion Michael felt for Cindy in his expression as he told her story.

"Fortunately, Cindy had an opportunity to accept the true Jesus Christ into her life when she was young. God had planned a strategy for her freedom from the darkness since the beginning of time. This strategy went into full motion when she chose Him to be her Lord and Savior.

"God began bringing people into her path here and there who could give her a reprieve from her pain. He brought her a school teacher who showed great compassion toward her on her most difficult days and a Sunday School teacher who interceded for Cindy throughout the week.

"Heaven wanted nothing more than to rescue her from her biological family, but the claims that Satan had on her needed to be addressed first. There was simply no one with spiritual authority in her life who was willing to break them for her. God gave her parents many opportunities to choose Him and to make better choices for Cindy. Although there were moments where they seemed to respond, it never lasted. Ultimately, God had to wait until Cindy was old enough to have full spiritual authority over her own life. Then the claims Satan had over her could be easily broken."

Michael paused as he felt the wind of a demon come hurtling through the room as if hit by a wrecking ball. The demon hit the adjacent wall and was gone as quickly as he came. Michael smiled and continued.

"God has been guiding her toward freedom every day since then. Today, we are in for a real victory."

Michael smiled with the confidence of someone who had witnessed the power and authority of the Most High God for hundreds of years. His smile could not be seen in the darkness surrounding the angelic warriors, but the confidence behind his smile could be easily felt.

For a moment, Gabe thought he felt the darkness tremble just slightly.

On the other side of the invisible shield and settled in her big chair, Mary addressed God in the heavenly courtroom. The three mighty warriors turned their attention to the conversation. They could see the courtroom and both of the ladies sitting in front of them in a separate dimension. The Most High God had gathered the group of powers and principalities that would be dealt with today. Within this unseen spirit world, a tall, cosmic being—a spirit of death—was also standing before the Judge Over All Things. God allowed Mary and Cindy to see and experience this spiritual place in their mind's eye.

Hundreds of demons in service to this mighty spirit fought and raged in the darkness surrounding the warriors and outside of the office. The sound of metal hitting metal with great force was deafening at times. The darkness in the room was so intense, Cindy squirmed and itched with fear and anxiety. She had lived with a spirit of death ruling her life for as long as she could remember. It was all she knew. Today, that spirit was being called out, and as much as she wanted to be free, it was a scary, scary thought.

Cindy refocused internally and looked at the image of the courtroom the Lord had placed in her mind. She noticed the evil being at the defendant's table appeared confident and unwavering in his expression. A legion of his followers swarmed behind him in the courtroom. As the spirit of death described his claim to Cindy's life, his arrogance sent a shiver down her spine. Cindy was all too familiar with his presence; she had sensed it her entire life. It had never been this clear, though. His claims were solid, and Cindy was unsure what Father God would say.

As the being ended his monologue, snickering could be heard from the swarm at the back of the courtroom.

Mary cleared her throat and began, "Cindy, do you choose to forgive your ancestors and the others involved for opening the door to this being both in your bloodline and in your personal life?"

"I do."

Cindy had prayed this prayer with Mary many times before over a variety of claims against her. Although she was nervous, feeling the evil so close, she trusted Mary to walk her through the steps of freedom, and she trusted Father God to bring about the freedom.

"Cindy, do you choose to belong to this evil being or the Most High God?"

"I choose to only belong to the Most High God." That one was easy.

"Most High God, the Judge and Ruler over all things," Mary began, "You know that Cindy was not given a choice in this matter. You hear her choice today to forgive those involved in making a covenant with this spirit, and You hear her choice to only belong to You, the Most High God. I ask, based on her forgiveness and her free will choice, that You would sever the claim this being has on her and that any penalty for breaking this covenant would be met by the death and resurrection of the true Jesus Christ."

As Mary continued to pray, Ronan, Gabe, and Michael watched as Father God evicted the spirit of death from Cindy's life. A huge sword glowing with the power of the Holy Spirit and crafted by the power of Christ's resurrection sliced through the cord of steel woven into Cindy's family line and completely severed it. Shards of steel flew in every direction, disintegrating into thin air and leaving no trace behind. Screams could be heard from the demonic warriors in and around the office. The warriors watched as the darkness in Mary's office began to swirl. Frantic cries came from the beings as they were sucked out the doors and windows into nothingness.

The three guardians could hear the battle outside as the warriors on the perimeter fought the lingering and defiant spirits to keep them from remaining on the property or near the office. They knew Mary's trust in God to protect her office fully equipped the angelic army to handle the battle outside of the office. The warriors' presence in the office kept the demonic beings obedient to the restrictions placed around Mary and Cindy.

The women agreed in prayer for a few more minutes, and afterward, the room was calm and bright again, both spiritually and to the natural eye as well. Ronan raised his sword to the Father. "Honor and power be to the Most High God!"

Gabe and Michael followed his lead, unsheathing and raising their swords as well. "Honor and power be to the Most High!"

A tear rolled down Cindy's cheek. "I never knew the weight I carried with that spirit until this very moment." Her eyes were staring at the floor, trying to make sense of the change she was experiencing. "It has always been there; I thought it was just a part of me. I didn't know I could feel this way. I didn't know there was anything different."

Mary smiled. "God's power is so great. He wants to bring each of us freedom in so many ways. You may be surprised at how different this next week feels."

"All of my life," Cindy responded, "I have had people tell me that I just need to believe more or read my Bible more or do this or that." She paused, reviewing these experiences in her mind. "But I haven't been able to do any of that."

Mary nodded with an appreciation for Cindy's journey with the Lord.

"Don't get me wrong. I tried, I tried with all I had in me. I just couldn't. And I never knew why. I thought there was something wrong with me." Cindy stared at the painting of daisies on the wall behind Mary. "Now I know. This spirit has been suffocating me, making it impossible, really, for me to be a good Christian."

Mary sat quietly, waiting for Cindy to continue to put the pieces together.

"And now," Cindy started, "well, today, I didn't do anything. I barely go to church. I still don't read my Bible. And yet, God..." She struggled to put her emotions into words. "And yet, God did this for me. He just did it."

Mary nodded slowly, allowing the powerful truth of what had just happened to sink into Cindy's heart.

"Yes, He did, Cindy. He did it."

Worshipping angels were around the room singing praises to the Most High God for the mighty victory they had just witnessed, although only the angelic guard could hear it.

"I still don't understand what's happening to me, though," Cindy continued. "What is happening inside of my mind."

"I know. It's complicated." Mary's smile put Cindy at ease. "The trauma you experienced as a child split up your mind into these different compartments, different parts."

"Like the images of children I see in my head," Cindy stated.

"Yes! They are dissociated images of yourself from throughout your life. The parts of you that helped you survive as a child." Mary paused for a moment. "You see, the Lord knew that, alone, a child could not handle the type of trauma you survived, so in His divine mercy, He created an internal system that could split up your identity and allow you to be more than one person. Do more than one job. Believe contradicting and confusing things at the same time."

Cindy finished the statement she had heard Mary say many, many times before. "All so I could survive."

Mary nodded. "Each part of your identity that split from the whole is now represented in your mind by an image or a voice, sometimes a picture of some kind. These parts hold memories from the past, and some help you do your daily tasks. The Lord is working to heal them and bring them all back together again—the way He originally designed."

Cindy gave Mary a weak smile. "I know. I am grateful; really, I am." She sighed. "I still just don't understand."

"It's okay, Cindy, you don't need to understand for God to do the work. Just trust Him." Mary cautiously added, "Did you want to talk about tomorrow before you go?"

Cindy's body stiffened. "No, I can't."

Mary knew Cindy was at her limit. She gave her a reassuring nod and then bowed her head to pray the wrap-up prayer.

As they ended the session, Michael prepared his small band of angelic servants to leave with Cindy. While Michael had enjoyed being in the glory of the Lord at Mary's office, he knew the shift that would be coming. Michael knew Cindy well. He knew her dissociation. He knew that there were more battles left to fight. The unseen internal world was filled with pain, sorrow, and wounds that still needed healing. God was with them, but still, the work was hard on Cindy.

"Gabe," Ronan stated.

"Yes, sir."

"Go with Michael for the week. Observe his charge. You will learn a great deal about the battle you are being trained to face."

"Yes, sir!" Gabe quickly fell into the ranks behind Michael.

As Cindy got in her car and started her long drive home, she still reveled in the difference she felt. The air felt lighter, and somehow even the sun felt brighter and warmer on her face. She took a deep breath, held it for a moment, and then let it out with a smile.

During her time in the heavenly courtroom, she had felt many dissociated parts of herself come together or integrate into a deep area of her heart. She had to remind herself of the truths Mary told her often. It felt good to have the Lord heal in this way. She was feeling more and more complete every day. Cindy longed for complete healing, but on days like this, she felt so close to finally being whole that it was almost painful to think of still dissociating.

The airy freedom she had experienced in Mary's office lasted for the rest of the day. It felt so good.

That night, when Cindy went to bed, she thought for sure she would have a good night's sleep in the new peace she had found. She fell asleep quickly, but her sleep was restless. Her dreams were filled with random images and emotions. Michael could sense her growing restlessness and instructed Rabok, one of the two ministering angels who were part of his angelic guard, to intervene. As he did, a bright light entered Cindy's dreams blocking out all images, and she awoke with a start.

"Three a.m.," she muttered as she looked at her phone. She saw a text she had sent to Mary around midnight:

We are so sad. We want Jesus to help us too.

It was not uncommon for Cindy to find texts and emails that she had sent with no memory of having sent them. She shrugged it off. She could tell she was not going back to sleep, so she got up, put on her robe, and headed into the kitchen. A single lightbulb in the small light fixture dimly lighted the kitchen. A few dishes were cluttered over the counter, and a Styrofoam box with her leftovers from two nights ago was on the table. Her body went through the motions of making tea.

"What happened in session yesterday?" she asked herself.

Was session yesterday?

Yes, yes, I think it was.

What happened?

The teapot began to rustle on the stovetop.

The spirit of death, that's right. We were in the courtroom. God did...something...

Cindy's mind went blank.

The teapot whistled loudly, startling her out of her thoughts.

Rabok stood nearby as Cindy poured a cup of tea and headed into the living room. While her mind flowed here and there with the thoughts of yesterday's session, Rabok was speaking words of life to her spirit. The words kept her grounded. They kept her from floating off into the nothingness that was grabbing at her mind.

Cindy was trying to grasp the amazing feeling she knew she had experienced at the session but could not quite remember. Random thoughts about her job search and bills that were piling up swirled around. Her mind would not settle on one particular thought. It was a familiar endless dialogue that she barely tolerated.

Why can't I stay free? Why do I always have to slip back into this pain and sadness? What am I doing wrong?

She could feel tears trying to come, but they were being held back. By what, she did not know.

Rabok knew she needed to cry, but internal forces were restraining the tears. The true Holy Spirit empowered ministering angels to bring a sense of peace and rest to those in need. Salih, Rabok's companion, assisted Cindy in processing her feelings, but tonight, that would not be possible. Rabok knew that. He focused on allowing the peace of God to flow into the room so she could rest. He knew this was needed, especially after the intense session the day before.

Gabe watched as the angelic comforter knelt beside the couch where Cindy was wrapped up in a blanket.

His frame was strong but much smaller than Michael and Ronan's warrior-like presence. He rarely spoke unless he was speaking life and peace to his charge. His demeanor was gentle, but he carried an authority to impart the presence of the Lord that could not be rivaled. His presence could be felt by every person and spiritual entity he encountered. The peace he had been equipped to carry to people was powerful. He spread his large, silver wings over Cindy and surrounded her with the peace of God.

Cindy glanced at her phone one more time at 5 a.m. She whispered a prayer for protection and drifted off to sleep.

Rabok stayed by Cindy as she slept. Her mind was still active, but he knew she would not remember the dreams or be kept awake by them. She needed rest now, just rest.

Two angelic warriors, Kaleb and Hezek, were cornering a handful of demonic spirits to the left of the small living room.

"You'll never survive," one spirit hissed toward Cindy with vile spit shooting from his lips.

"Useless, you're just useless!" the other one spouted off.

They did not acknowledge Kaleb and Hezek, but they did not attempt to move past them either.

The warriors knew the demons were not close enough to where Cindy was sleeping to influence her. She had prayed as she fell asleep that God would prohibit Satan from interfering with her sleep. These demons could not cross that prayer.

"If the demons can't bother Cindy, why is there still such a battle?" Gabe asked as he walked to Michael's side.

"The demons have been held at bay for the moment, but Cindy still has to deal with the internal war and horrors that plague her story. Her childhood trauma split her thoughts and feelings into separate pieces. There is still room between these pieces for these spirits to harass."

Gabe remembered that Mary, Cindy's therapist, had called these splits self-images or parts.

"The splits are Cindy, but in pieces," Michael continued. "She experiences these pieces in her mind as images of herself throughout her life. Little girl images who had experienced pain, teen images who had fought their way through high school and family expectations, and even other adult images who were trying desperately to improve her quality of life," Michael paused as Gabe took in the information. "These images hold her memories, feel her emotions, and live her life. It's part of God's design for survival."

"I have never experienced anything like this before," Gabe said with genuine awe of the Creator.

"It is truly an amazing design." Michael glanced at Cindy. His strong arms were resting at his side, and confidence in the Creator's design was on his face. "Right now, she is at the stage of healing where she is experiencing the conflict internally that has been buried for so many years."

Gabe was beginning to understand. "So, as she becomes more aware of these pieces of her identity, she feels the pain they carry as well."

Michael nodded. "As she heals, she becomes more and more aware of the conflict inside. The war is deep in Cindy's subconscious mind, and she only had a vague awareness of it until now. Most of the time, she doesn't even know why she is fighting. She only knows she is fighting for survival." Michael sighed and looked back at Cindy, who was now deep in sleep, "Rabok is good at his work. Cindy's sleep will be full of internal activity, but at least she will get some rest."

Gabe nodded in agreement.

And rest was needed for her to get through what was coming on Friday.

Chapter 2

Beams from the morning sun streamed into Cindy's bedroom as she rolled over and opened her eyes. Cindy had dreaded this day for the last month. She feared it was a day she would not survive. She spent longer in bed than she wanted, but when she looked at the clock and saw it was 10 a.m., she knew she had to move, or she would be late. Being late would have even worse consequences than going would. Cindy winced at the thought. Just then, a shift, sudden but gentle. A different part of her mind had taken over, shifting her perspective and mood. With robotic-like motions, she swung her feet off the bed and onto the floor. Mindlessly, she ran her fingers through her hair and swept it up in a ponytail as she collected her clothes for the day. Thirty minutes later, she was showered, dressed, and headed out the door.

The drive was both long and not long enough. This would be her last visit to her parents' house; at least, that is what she had told her therapist. She needed to get away from them. Her mom was horrible to her as a child, and her dad was even worse. This was one of the few things her many self-images could agree on. Seeing her parents was unbearable, and going to the house was even worse. Today, it was necessary, though. It was her mother's birthday. There were obligations and expectations, and if she did not go, there would be hell to pay.

A tear streamed down her face. She ignored it. All she wanted was a mother who loved her and cared for her. Someone you associate with children's bedtime stories—the quaint little picture of a mom holding her blonde-haired, blue-eyed daughter in a rocking chair while reading her a story. They were usually snuggled under a warm blanket with a simple lamp nearby for the light. The picture was both beautiful and painful. She pushed it out of her head.

At least my parents live more than an hour away.
After today though, I have to set a boundary. I have to.
Boundaries are impossible. They never work.
I have to try.

As her little blue Toyota crossed over the property line of the family's old farmhouse, Michael could see the darkness in the air. Around the property, portals were open to many different spiritual domains. The air was thick as demons swirled in and out of the portals, growling at the car. Mocking laughter ran through the air, and a few insults were hurled in Michael's direction.

He did not respond. He knew the Most High God had put impenetrable protection around Cindy and her car, which would allow his guard to defeat any attacks successfully that came their way. Although her inner world tormented Cindy, and she could feel the darkness she was entering, she was safe from any harm from these spiritual pests.

Kaleb and Hezek were battling a few of the demons coming from portals that were still attached to Cindy. Their sword fight was swift and sure as the power of God's protection ran through them.

The rest of the angelic army, led by Michael, followed as Cindy's car bounced along the dirt road. She slowed as she got closer. The long driveway was lined with expensive cars. Undoubtedly, visitors trying to seem important and show off their status within the community. Cindy's stomach turned. A huge portal was open over the farmhouse. Hate, greed, and evil poured out of it. It was invisible to the natural eye, and most could not even sense its existence, but Cindy could. A few more warriors joined Michael as they approached the house.

"I think I'm going to be sick," Cindy muttered.

Her breath was slow and steady as she slid her car into a spot near the barn on the side of the house. *No one will block me in here*, she thought.

You are trapped just by being here, her mind retorted.

Shut up!

Michael issued assignments to the medium-sized group of angelic beings that were at his disposal for the day.

The front steps seemed taller than Cindy remembered. She could hear soft crying inside her mind. She blocked it out.

I remember this house, a small whimpering voice echoed through Cindy's mind.

I wish I could remember what happened here, Cindy thought. *I wish I knew why it feels so, so terrible.*

No, you don't, the voice responded.

The farmhouse was big but old. It had been in her family for years. Her grandfather had bought the house when he and her grandmother had first married. It was quite the show house back in the day. Elegant landscaping covered the front yard. Beautiful bushes lined the walkway to the front door, while rose bushes and other flowers were planted in various large planters along the full-wrap-around porch. Ten-foot marble pillars held up the porch roof, and fresh plants hung between each one.

Cindy heard stories of the grand parties her grandparents hosted on Sunday afternoons. Practically their whole church would come and picnic and socialize. She could remember the pressure her mother, Darlene, felt when Cindy was growing up. There was an expectation that Darlene would carry on the tradition of entertaining, but Darlene could never really live up to the expectations that came with the marriage and the house. Cindy remembered her mom in two ways: crying or angry. Both were equally scary. As she grew older, Cindy also remembered her mom with a mask. She wore it any time someone "outside" was around. Darlene would somehow transform into a social, happy housewife.

Stepford Mom, Cindy thought bitterly. That was who she would see today.

Cindy reached the door. She took a deep breath and held it for a moment. Her shoulders slumped to her side—another gentle but firm internal shift. A different self-image had taken over to move her forward. She grabbed the doorknob and pushed herself into the entry of the home.

She was dizzy, and the room seemed to be spinning around her. She could hear talking and laughing off in the distance. She focused hard on the sound, and slowly the room and sound came into focus.

"Yeah, I made a great deal on that old warehouse just five months ago! Business has been great!"

"Really? I had no idea you were such a businessman!"

Various conversations trailed around her as she began to feel herself walking through the room.

"When did you get back from Europe?"

"Just a few days ago. It was so amazing! Here, let me show you some of the pictures I took."

Cindy was glad everyone was engaged in conversation. It allowed her to make her way through the room in a silent fashion. It looked like a good turnout. There were about fifty people there so far—all important, all wealthy. Music streamed from the living room. It was an upbeat tune, but it sounded hollow to Cindy. A few people greeted her as she passed through the entry, down the hall, and into the kitchen. Her parents would always hire the best caterers and service people to help with the party to keep up appearances. She knew she would find something good to eat.

She ignored the elaborate birthday cake as she entered the kitchen and headed for the kitchen island, where half a dozen trays of appetizers were awaiting delivery. She still felt quite nauseous but found herself stuffing a few parmesan pastry puffs in her mouth.

"Her routine is always the same," Michael said to Gabe. "She will stick to the kitchen and the back patio, with occasional trips to the bathroom to catch her breath and help settle her mind."

Gabe looked around. "It seems the additional troops you requested for the day have all arrived."

Three warriors were stationed outside, three warriors in the kitchen, and Rabok and Salih near the bathroom, for those times when Cindy was feeling overwhelmed and needed to retreat. The rest of the team was stationed around the property, enforcing God's boundaries against the open portals.

"I have never seen so many open portals around one home!" Gabe commented as he surveyed the property.

"Cindy's family has been opening them for many generations." Michael was solemn. "Her great, great grandfather started it when he fell into greed and lust for power. With each new generation, the curses and spiritual bondage he came into agreement with have increased and become more and more entangled in this bloodline."

"I don't see how any child could survive in a home like this."

"No child could, at least, not without the help of the Lord."

"But each of these portals would have access to Cindy?"

"Yes, they did have access to her. What happened in this house and with permission of Cindy's parents was incomprehensible. The abuse threatened to take her life. If it weren't for the careful strategy of God to prepare a way of escape for her, she would either be serving the gods of these portals or completely insane." Michael looked toward the heavens. "But God, in His sovereignty, allowed Cindy to dissociate and survive the unthinkable in a way that would keep her core self both safe and hidden. This system allowed Cindy's humanity to be preserved until she could choose on her own who to serve. The mental health world calls it 'dissociation,' but Cindy only knows it as her life. She is beginning to see the Lord's design in it."

"Why did no one get her out?"

"No one could." Michael was solemn. "But God. God brought her to the attention of random strangers who would then intercede for her in prayer for days and sometimes weeks. She accepted the Lord into her heart when she was nine years old, and that gave us more access to intervene on her behalf, but her parents were still in control of her daily life. There were a few families in the neighborhood who God used to offer her refuge on an occasional afternoon or evening."

Michael smiled. "Then, as soon as Cindy was of age to have full spiritual authority in her life, her Father God offered her an opportunity to choose Him fully, and she did. She chose the Most High God to rescue her. Since then, I have had full access to her. I have fought for her, grieved with her, rejoiced with her, and been by her side every day."

"That's amazing. God is amazing."

The two stood in awe for a moment.

Michael continued, "The work to free her from this poisoned bloodline is great. The battle has been intense, but His power is more than enough to break off the strongholds that have been consuming this family line for generations!"

Gabe glanced toward Hezek, one of the warriors stationed by the kitchen door. His stature was tall compared to Cindy and the waitstaff in the room. His stance was firm, but his attention had turned toward the entrance to the living room, and his hand was on his sword.

Cindy's mother walked through the doorway. A swirl of hissing, angry demons surrounded Darlene. They noted Hezek's gaze and momentarily silenced their comments.

"Hi, sweetie." Darlene's voice felt like sugar-laced poison.

Cindy choked.

"Someone said they saw you come in." Darlene walked up behind her daughter and squeezed her shoulder in a half-hug sort of way. "I should have known you would be in the kitchen."

The pack of demons chuckled with laughter.

Hezek took a half-step forward with his hand still on his sword.

The demons quieted.

Cindy cringed. It took less than two minutes for her mother to make a dig at her weight.

"Hi, mother." She could feel the cheese puffs she had just eaten, trying to make a reappearance. "Happy birthday."

As the words left her mouth, she felt nauseous and then dizzy.

Michael sent Jamison and Tritok, two warrior angels, to her side and one to walk in front and one behind. Jamison was a regular reinforcement on days like this, but Tritok was new. He was a huge warrior with dark skin and deep brown eyes. He had been sent because of his special experience with the evils of ritual abuse. While Cindy was safe from the serious harm of the demons in the room, the emotional pain being triggered in her heart was pretty overwhelming. Michael signaled, and Salih joined them at Cindy's side to help her manage her heart.

"Be sure these trays reach our guests before they are cold," Darlene instructed the waitstaff.

Cindy stood at the kitchen island, trying to look casual as she watched her mother flitter around giving orders and tasting the food to make sure it measured up to some unknown standard. Cindy knew if she left right away, her mother would be offended, but it was all she could do to stand there.

"Why doesn't she just leave?" Gabe questioned.

Most of the demons in the room had determined by now that Hezek and the others were not there to bother them, so the evil chatter was beginning again.

"A long time ago, Cindy determined in her heart that she had to be loyal to her parents to minimize the abuse she received from them."

"Did it work?" Gabe asked.

"To a degree. It lessened punishments for disloyalty, and occasionally it allowed Cindy to know what they expected of her before it became an issue."

"But why does she stay loyal to them now? She could move to another country and never talk to them again if she wanted."

"It's not that simple. Those parts of Cindy's heart are sworn to protect her through this loyalty. It would seem like the ultimate self-betrayal to give that up."

"She must be in torment."

"She is," Michael affirmed. "Her parts are helping her, and Salih is bringing comfort to strengthen her as well."

Cindy let her gaze wander into the living room just off the kitchen. Janice Smith and Kathy Brine were two social queens in the small town her parents were from. They were having their usual subtle bragging conversations.

"The light from these French doors is exquisite!" Janice gushed. "It reminds me so much of my time in

Italy." She sighed as her eyes drifted away for a moment. "The skylights in the museums were amazing!"

"Oh, I can only imagine!" Kathy responded with equals amounts of gushing. "Unfortunately, we didn't make it to Italy this year. We were busy taking a tour of the Holy Land. Israel is so beautiful, and, of course, it is where Jesus walked." She smiled as her eyes met Janice's. "We walked on the same ground as our Lord. I would call that divine."

Demons of comparison, pride, and low self-esteem swarmed the ladies. Snickers and small daggers were being thrown at each of them as if it were some game.

A group of teenagers was gathered on the plush sofas and chairs in similar conversations across the room. An arrogant and judgmental spirit was hovering close, and pride and deception took turns nudging the teens into their conversation.

"Why, I have never even seen so many run-down homes in my life!" Susan, a blonde-haired girl about sixteen, was saying, "My mom says we should be grateful we don't have to live like they do."

"Weren't you driving through the new development out east of town?" questioned a tan, brown-eyed boy about the same age.

"New?" she scoffed. "I don't think so! Most of those homes are at least ten years old! I wouldn't be caught dead living there!"

Cindy shook her head as she passed by the teens and made her way out the side door to the backyard.

On the patio, four of the more prominent figures in the community were gathered to talk about religion and politics. She cringed at their use of Scripture to justify their judgmental attitudes.

Lies and deception danced around another group of young adults, presumably children of some of the adults present, as they spun tales of magic, power, and insecurity.

Cindy kept walking. She could feel the evil everywhere, and it made her skin crawl.

Several other groups scattered about the property had their own selection of demons plaguing the guests with whatever trouble and influence they were allowed.

"It's no wonder Cindy had so many battles given this home where she was raised," Gabe commented.

Cindy had been in therapy for years working through her childhood trauma, and she had learned a lot of tools necessary to build a stable life for herself. But since she had begun meeting with Mary, her healing journey had taken a major turn. She engaged in serious spiritual warfare, breaking off many of the strongholds and bondages that kept her from experiencing true freedom. This journey had come to the point that she needed to break off all physical attachments to her parents, as well as the spiritual ones. While Cindy desperately wanted never to see them again, the parts of her identity that were loyal to her parents, and the parts who still loved her parents, were not so agreeable to the needed boundary.

"Looks like Cindy made it to the backyard," Gabe noted.

"There is more space here. She'll feel less confined."

Michael glanced around. Each warrior was at his post. There was a clear view of the huge portal hovering above the home, and the warriors all had swords drawn. Some were engaged in battle with the enemy; others were standing their ground near Cindy, ready to act quickly if needed. The day would be intense, but they would win. Cindy would be protected from any spiritual assault here. Michael was sure of that.

Cindy was headed for a hammock just off the back porch. That was her spot. *If I can just sit here, unnoticed for the rest of the party, I will be okay,* Cindy thought.

"There you are!" It was her dad. "I have been looking for you." He said with a fake smile that made her stomach turn. A tall, evil being followed him as he crossed the yard to his daughter.

There was a man with him. He was a little taller than her dad, darker. Cindy felt a moment of confusion as her dad said, "You remember my friend Tom." An angel swooped down with a fiery sword and made a deadly stab against a burly demon headed for Cindy's head.

The demon thudded just out of sight and evaporated into the air. The tall, demonic being with her father either didn't notice or didn't care.

* * *

"I don't really remember much," Cindy heard herself saying as Mary's face began to come into focus. She realized she was in Mary's office.

It must be Thursday, she thought.

"What is the last thing you remember?" Mary was asking with a gentle tone.

"I'm not really sure." Cindy thought hard. She could hear many things in her head, but none of them made sense.

"You had your mother's birthday party last week, didn't you?" Mary asked slowly. "Stay with me if you can."

Cindy's mind had started to drift away, but she forced herself to stay present at the request of her therapist.

"How did that go?"

"I remember driving up that long driveway; then, I'm not sure." Cindy was frustrated with herself. Why was she unable to remember something so simple? You would think a party would have at least stuck in her head a little. She was sure there was some good food there. For a split second, Tom's face flashed in her mind; then it was gone.

"I'm sorry, I just don't remember anything between driving up that painfully long driveway and sitting here with you."

"That's okay," her therapist assured her. "I know how unsettling that is."

Cindy felt numb. "I don't know. I guess it's just my life. Is it Thursday?"

"It is," Mary responded.

"And the party was Friday?"

"I believe it was," Mary confirmed.

"So, I lost the whole week," Cindy said more to herself than to Mary.

Idiot, how can you lose a whole week!

"I don't like that," Cindy said as she pulled her knees up to her chin. She wrapped her arms around her legs. Her face looked young. She looked to be about eight years old and very sad.

"I know you don't," Mary said with kindness in her voice. "It's hard not to know what is happening in your own life."

"People don't understand, but you do."

"I try to." Mary gave a small smile.

"Sometimes, I don't even understand myself." Cindy was moving one of her hands to feel the texture on the couch cushions as she talked. "I mean, how can I forget so much? How can I be living, and eating, and sleeping, and just not remember? I wish I weren't dissociated. If I didn't have parts, life would be so much easier."

"Maybe. But sometimes life can be so overwhelming that it is easier not to remember." Mary waited until Cindy looked up, and their eyes met. "Is that what happened? Did something overwhelming happen at the party that made you forget?"

The question was gentle enough but still too much for Cindy to take. Her feet dropped back to the floor, and her face seemed to age back to adulthood right before Mary's eyes.

"I don't know. I just don't know."

"That's okay. We can talk about something else." Mary turned a page in her notebook. "Are you still desiring to set some boundaries with your parents?"

There was the dizzy again. Cindy pushed through.

"I *have* to."

Mary nodded in agreement. "Let's pray about it."

Mary began her courtroom prayer.

Ronan, Michael, and Gabe had been standing in their usual spots with their team stationed in and around the office. Rabok was nearby, and Salih was sitting close to Cindy to help her manage the flood of emotions that he could sense just behind a wall in her heart. They all knew the impact of going into the Lord's courtroom, and their spiritual enemy knew it too. The angelic army drew their swords. They, along with the many angels covering the space, felt an unusual shake in the room. A portal was opening.

"Father God," Mary began, "it is a great honor to be allowed into Your heavenly courtroom. Please block the path to the enemy's counterfeit courtroom, and allow our case to be heard before You, Most High God."

Cindy's shoulders flinched and then relaxed. "I can see the courtroom," she said with her eyes closed. "The Judge is at the front behind a big table."

"Where are you?" Mary asked as she jotted down a few notes.

"I can see myself standing on the left side of the courtroom. Jesus is with me."

"Good." Mary turned back to prayer, "Father God, would You please bring the evil keeping Cindy in bondage to her birth family into Your courtroom."

The room grew darker as evil began to pour from the open portal. Cindy winced and squeezed her eyes tighter. "They are coming in."

Ronan and the others could hear the clash of swords. The scuffle of good and evil fighting around the perimeter of the office was getting louder, closer. The portal was now fully open above the office, and a stream of demonic entities was flooding the space. The steam from their presence would be suffocating to a human. Ronan was not affected by it, but even still, he did not like it.

He slashed his sword through a trio of demons, trying to escape the pull into the courtroom.

Michael turned to Gabe. "This particular portal has been connected to Cindy since before she was born. A few months ago, the Lord blocked it so it could not influence Cindy anymore, but it is still connected to her," he explained.

"Closed, but still connected?" Gabe questioned as he herded a few dark stragglers into the flow toward the heavenly courtroom.

Michael nodded toward Ronan to explain so he could check the progress outside of the office. Kaleb followed.

"Yes," Ronan began, "you see, there are many, many ways that Satan tries to keep people in bondage."

The flow from the portal was now thick in the room, but the evil could not pull away from the Lord's command to enter the courtroom. The darkness gushed from the open portal and was immediately pulled into the heavenly realm where the Lord's courtroom existed. Ronan and Gabe stood at the edge, ready to engage if needed.

"Satan has leverage when he can trick or coerce someone into giving him permission to connect to their lives." Ronan knew Gabe must understand these principles if he were to advance in the Lord's army. "Satan is allowed to influence people in a variety of ways, but people give him permission to connect with them through agreements with lies, generational curses, personal sin, and a few other ways."

The stream was thinning now. Hezek kept a close eye on Mary and Cindy as the flow of evil moved past them.

"Why would anyone agree to these things?" Gabe had not been assigned to Mary's team long, but he had been there long enough to know that every client wanted desperately to be free from Satan's grip. It was difficult to understand how they would have permitted him to keep them in bondage.

"It is simple," Michael responded. "Satan is a liar, a deceiver, and a counterfeiter of truth. He tricks people into giving permission, and, in the case of Cindy and those like her, he forces them to give permission through evil and abusive means."

Gabe nodded. It made sense that people would not usually give permission knowingly or easily. Knowing the adversary as he did, it made sense that he would take advantage of every weakness in humanity to try to get their permission. After all, his purpose was to kill, steal, and destroy everything belonging to the Most High God. Every person, plant, and animal—all of Creation—fell in that category.

The evil stream from the open portal had stopped completely now. The courtroom was filled with fluid darkness moving and hissing with steady movements.

"We must be severing the connection to this portal today," Michael said just under his breath as he reentered the room.

Ronan nodded in agreement, and the three angelic warriors turned their attention toward Mary and Cindy sitting on the couch in the small office. They could see in both dimensions: the heavenly courtroom and the small-town therapy office. The contrast between the two was stark, but the connection was solid.

The huge portal expanded briefly so a tall cosmic being could enter the room, holding an old scroll in his huge hand. At first glance, he was dressed in brilliant white. His demeanor was confident. His stride was smooth, with a sense of ownership in each step. As the being approached the bench where the Judge Over All Things sat, the being's robe began to look dingy in the presence of the Most High God. This did not impact the being's confidence.

Behind the evil being, the fluid movement of demonic beings slowed, waiting to hear what would be said.

"She is mine," the cosmic being pronounced before the Holy Judge. "And she always will be."

Cindy shuddered at his claim, and Michael's angelic force stood on guard, acting as bailiffs in the heavenly courtroom. While there were legal grounds to be addressed, the evil was only allowed so much leeway in the process. Still, demons were hissing and spitting toward Cindy.

"What is your claim to Cindy?" Mary asked with authority in her voice.

The Holy Judge looked at the cosmic being. A slight grin crept across the face of the being, and he looked as though he was remembering something.

"Many generations ago, a covenant was made for her life." He continued with details about the covenant and who was involved.

Cindy's body was tight. She could hear the being giving the account of the transaction. In her mind's eye, she could still see the heavenly courtroom, although she didn't really want to.

"I know it is easy for the evil to draw your attention, but try focusing on God instead," Mary encouraged.

Cindy complied. The Most High God sat behind his bench, patiently listening. He had a strong but peaceful demeanor. He was like a rock, immoveable in His role as judge and unshaken by the confidence spewing from the evil being before Him. Cindy's body relaxed slightly.

Once she was able to feel the peace of God, her attention turned to the image of herself standing on the defendant's side of the courtroom. The self-image that represented Cindy was about four years old. She was dirty and dressed in rags. Her face was down, and she was holding a small infant. Only Jesus stood between her and the evil cosmic being stating His ownership of her.

The little one glanced up at the Judge. Even though she was so small in His presence, she felt a sense of safety there. The Judge quickly glanced at her and gave a playful wink. Then He turned His calm but authoritative face back to the evil cosmic being.

The Judge raised His hand to silence the being. His intent was clear. He didn't use words, yet His instructions seemed to echo through the courtroom. The being was quiet, but the Judge's authority did not faze him.

Other than a few rebel demons being corralled in the back by angelic court attendants, the courtroom was still, quiet. Cindy sat nervously in Mary's office, unsure what to do. She had been in the courtroom many times before, but today seemed different somehow.

"Get ready," Ronan said to Gabe. "The small ones can be unruly once the Judge has ruled."

Gabe took a spot next to Hezek and closer to Mary to keep her protected from any backlash after the Judge's ruling.

"Cindy," Mary started softly, "are you ready to have the Most High God take care of this?"

With her eyes still pinched shut, Cindy nodded.

The evil cosmic being chuckled with arrogance, clearly mocking Cindy's choice.

"Cindy," Mary started with only a hint of her authority being heard in her voice, "do you choose to forgive your ancestors who initiated or participated in the covenant giving this being ownership of you and your future generations?"

Cindy nodded again, more slowly than the first time.

The evil cosmic being grew a little, and Cindy's small image pulled in a little closer to Jesus.

"Do you ask for forgiveness for any way in which you have knowingly or unknowingly come into agreement with this evil being over your life?"

Cindy nodded again with a bit more confidence.

"And do you desire to have him gone from your life?"

The evil being in the courtroom narrowed his eyes on Cindy, and she could feel the heat rising in her body. Oh, how she wanted freedom! Just being so close to him, she realized how much he had impacted her throughout her life. His presence was very familiar to her, and it was frightening. She absolutely wanted it gone, but she had difficulty believing it was even possible. She thought of all of the times she has sensed this being, not knowing what it was.

Terrible thoughts began to flood Cindy's mind.

"God, I ask You to silence any voices that are not of You." Mary prayed with full authority.

At that, a swirl of demons was revealed in the office, whispering in Cindy's ear. Hezek did not hesitate. With precision, he slashed through the entire pack with one blow.

"I do!" Cindy almost yelled it, and the demons tumbled away into red vapors. The evil being in the courtroom was instantly knocked into his chair. "I want him gone!" she confirmed.

"Father God, Judge Over All Things, based on Cindy's forgiveness, repentance, and free will choice today, I ask that you release Cindy from the ownership of this being and pronounce judgment against him."

The evil being started to rise against the ruling, but he could not. He could not even stand in the presence of the Judge.

Hezek, Kaleb, and the others were clearing the office of the demons who had tagged along with the evil being.

"I ask that the death and resurrection of Jesus Christ would cover any penalty for breaking this covenant," Mary added.

With that, the document that the being was holding burst into a flame and was gone instantly. The evil being gave one last growl before he was snatched from the courtroom. The sword of the Lord God came through the air like lightning and severed the cord that connected Cindy to the portal where the evil being had entered the room. As it was severed, the portal began to close. The evil being was escorted back to the portal, and demons of all sizes started swirling and scampering around the courtroom.

Some ran straight back into the portal. Some tried to escape by other means, but Michael, Ronan, and their troops kept them all herded toward the rapidly closing portal. As the last demon was thrown in, the portal closed with a final puff of smoke.

It was over.

Cindy let out a long breath she had not realized she was holding.

Is it really over? she questioned in her heart.

She knew it was. It was more than a feeling. It was a knowing. The Holy Spirit reassured her that this being was banished from her life forever.

Cindy noticed in her mind's eye that Jesus was now holding the little girl who was in the courtroom. She was clean now but still in rags. Her head rested peacefully on Jesus's shoulder, and she was still holding the infant. Jesus began to move away with them in His arms. Cindy knew they were going to the healing place the Lord had created for her at the beginning of her journey.

At that, Jesus disappeared from Cindy's mind's eye and into a place deep in her heart. The image of the courtroom faded as well, and Cindy was left with a sense of peace. As she relayed the experience to Mary, she thought of all of the times she had seen Jesus heal her self-images.

"Are you concerned about the little ones?" Mary asked.

"No," Cindy replied, "I know Jesus will take good care of them, I mean, of me. I never really know how to say that." She shot a nervous grin at her therapist, and they both smiled.

"I know it's complicated, but you have really done great work cooperating with the Lord on this confusing and often difficult journey."

Mary's affirmation felt good but was hard to accept. "I try," was all Cindy could say.

After a moment of contemplation, Cindy asked, "How do you do it?"

"Do what?"

"How do you fight such terrible, awful things and still look so, so peaceful?"

A small smile came over Mary's face. Her eyes softened slightly, and she leaned a little toward Cindy. "It's simple. I know the Judge."

"I want to know Him that way," Cindy mused. "I want to know Him so well that I don't shiver in fear when those terrible beasts show up!"

"You can, Cindy. God lives in your heart. He loves you very much, and He would love to spend time with you." Mary paused. "Would you like to talk to Him a little now?"

Cindy thought for a moment. While she was a little envious of Mary's relationship with the Holy Trinity, she was unsure whether they would respond to her the same way. Sure, she had experienced many wonderful moments with each of them, but it was all in the context of healing, not just talking. She was not sure if she was ready to find out how they really felt about her.

"Not today," Cindy responded. "I am pretty tired."

"That's okay. He will be there whenever you are ready." Mary relaxed back into her chair. "Do you want to talk about the court hearing that is coming up?"

Cindy's heart sank. "No, I just want to get it over with."

"Okay, we can process what happens in our next session." Mary's tone was pleasant, which allowed Cindy to relax again. Mary gave Cindy a few more minutes to talk about the events of the last hour.

As the session came to an end, Michael, Ronan, and the others stood by while Mary prayed a closing prayer for the session. Michael could sense a few spirits leaving Cindy that had been sent to harass her. When Mary prayed for extra protection against any retaliation toward Cindy, Michael felt Mary's faith reach the Holy Spirit and strengthen him and his troops for what the week would bring.

"There is still much to be done, but today was significant," Michael said to Ronan as they were parting ways at the end of the session.

"Yes, it was," responded Ronan. "Praise be to the Most High God!" he declared.

"Praise be to the Most High!" Michael echoed. The worshipping angels, Zral and Abel, led the troops in worship as the band of mighty angels followed Cindy to her car.

Chapter 3

A few days went by before Cindy took the time to think about the last session. She could sense more awareness of her own thoughts and feelings, which was both good and bad. She was also beginning to feel more present in her day-to-day life. More engaged, just a little bit.

Today she was trying something new. She was preparing to go for coffee with Angela, her pastor's wife. While staring into her closet, trying to find the best thing to wear, she debated whether or not to tell Angela about her dissociation. Meeting for coffee with someone she barely knew and telling someone about her dissociation would both be firsts for her. Her confidence had increased just enough that she thought they might be possible. Cindy longed for others to know her, the real her, but she didn't even know the real her, so she felt quite an internal conflict. Her mind began thinking through the idea of being honest with Angela about how the trauma had split her into many different parts.

I want Angela to know about my parts. She seems so kind and loving.

She would never understand.

She might. She seems so nice.

She might also think you're crazy.

Then an unfamiliar voice whispered from deep within Cindy's heart. *I just want her to hold me.*

Cindy froze, startled by that thought.

You are a grown adult! You don't need anyone to hold you! Don't be so foolish.

Cindy dropped her head slightly as a tinge of shame hit her heart.

I won't tell her. Today is not the day.

One day this dissociation will be gone, and I will finally be free. Then, I won't have to worry about telling anyone else ever again.

She finished getting ready and headed to the car as her mind continued to swirl with endless thoughts and conversation. She had learned from Mary that these racing thoughts were just parts of her identity, having ongoing conversations within her mind. Knowing this did not help her sort it out, though.

While she was driving, Michael was nearby. He had sent Kaleb and Hezek ahead to scout out the coffee shop to make sure it was all clear. Michael kept a close perimeter on all of Cindy's goings. Once or twice Cindy had been headed someplace her mother or father were just leaving. In those cases, Michael would gently divert Cindy to keep her from bumping into them unexpectedly.

As Cindy drove, Kaleb returned with a report for his leader.

"The coffee shop is clear of her parents or anyone who would be triggering." Kaleb stood at attention, waiting for Michael's response.

"Good." Michael nodded.

"Angela is already there," Kaleb reported in his no-nonsense way.

"How does she seem?" Michael wanted to prepare Cindy's heart for what might be coming.

"Calm, confident," Kaleb replied.

"And?" Michael could tell there was something more that Kaleb wanted to say.

"It was strange," he started. "As Angela arrived at the coffee house, there was a scuffle outside. A few harassing spirits tried to attack her as soon as she arrived. Two angelic warriors swooped out of nowhere, defeated them, and then vanished. I didn't recognize either one of them."

Michael looked past Kaleb as he nodded an acknowledgment and sent him on his way. "This will be an interesting visit."

Cindy pulled into the parking lot and parked in a particular spot so she could see inside the shop without Angela noticing her. She sat there and observed her pastor's wife for a moment. She was a younger woman—younger than Cindy anyways—probably in her late thirties. Her hair was long and perfectly combed, and she wore a casual shirt that hung neatly over her jeans.

She always looks so comfortable, some part of Cindy observed.

She would never understand you. Don't even try to talk to her about your problems. I don't even know why you agreed to this!

I just want someone to love me.

Stop it! Just stop it!

An invisible darkness began to settle over Cindy's car. Her body sank deep into the driver's seat, and she felt paralyzed.

Michael noticed her decline and was already taking action. There was no time to waste. The downward cycle of Cindy's state of mind had attracted the attention of a nearby spirit of hopelessness. Michael pulled his sword and jabbed through the darkness and into the roof of the little blue Toyota. Two of the nearby warriors saw him and immediately joined him, one at the front of the car and one at the rear.

Now, at least half a dozen demons were attempting to revel in the growing despair in the car.

Why try? Why even try?

Cindy's mind was shutting down.

Kaleb and Hezek took the front and back of the vehicle while Michael continued to wrestle with the dark spirit on the top, each stabbing their swords through the darkness and into the car. Three demons came hurtling out of the vehicle and vaporized.

There was a low rumble.

Cindy shivered. "Jesus, help!"

At Cindy's request for help, Michael's sword flashed with light, through the air and into the car's roof. "In the name of the Most High God, you must leave! You have no more place here!"

Two demons were speared through the side and disappeared in a puff of smoke. As the three warriors removed their swords from the vehicle, the darkness loosened and disappeared behind the building.

Cindy sat up and looked around. Her shoulders slowly straightened, and she checked around her as if she was lost.

Then, just as suddenly as the despair had hit, her mood shifted, and she relaxed. She casually checked her makeup in the mirror and then headed into the coffee shop.

"How does she do that?" Gabe asked in amazement. "One minute, she is sinking into the depths of hopeless despair, and the next, she is casually checking her makeup. I just don't understand."

"It's her system, Gabe, her dissociation. It allows her to shut off certain experiences or feelings when they become overwhelming. She quite literally just becomes someone different. Someone unaware of what just happened."

"This is a part of God's design?" Gabe was trying to understand, but it just felt so foreign and even artificial.

"Yes, it is. This ability to switch between the multiple parts of her brain—or shift as she sometimes calls it— is what allowed her to survive her childhood."

I guess I could see that, Gabe thought for a moment. "If this dissociation has been so helpful, then why would she want to change it?"

"It isn't helpful like it was in childhood. Now, the time she loses is important to her. She wants to be able to live every moment of her life."

Gabe nodded as he followed Michael and the others, still unsure if he completely understood.

The smell of coffee greeted Cindy as she opened the door to meet with Angela.

Once inside, Michael noticed a general in the angelic army posted behind Angela. He saw him regularly in passing at church services, but they had never officially met. They greeted each other with a nod. Angela's angelic band also gave Michael a non-verbal greeting, and the sound of the worshipping angels blended in with the songs of praise being sung by Angela's angelic guard.

The inside of the coffee shop was pleasant, almost cheerful. Quiet conversations could be heard around the room, and several teens played a board game in the back corner. Cindy was drawn toward the cozy fireplace near the back of the shop, but that wasn't the spot where Angela had chosen to sit.

As Cindy approached, Angela looked up from her coffee and smiled. Cindy's stomach flipped as Angela stood and gave her a hug that matched the cozy feeling of the fireplace.

"Good morning, Cindy! I'm so glad you could make it."

Cindy needed to feel loved and wanted it right now, but even the little bit she felt from Angela was almost more than she could handle.

Salih was right by Cindy's side. He knew she could not handle the full emotion of comfort, but the work of the Holy Spirit was evident in Salih's presence, allowing Cindy to receive some of the comfort despite her resistance to it. It was water to her soul and yet painful at the same time.

Why, why can't you just be normal?

Just sit down and get this over with.

Cindy sighed as she sat down. She just wanted to enjoy the morning. Why did she have to be tortured simply for having coffee?

She mustered a small smile. "Good morning."

Angela sat down. "Can I get you a coffee or a pastry? Something hot? They make excellent quiche here!"

"I'm fine, thanks." Cindy was unsure she could keep anything down, even if she tried.

I can't do this, she thought to herself. In a flash, she felt her body relax. A tiny bit more energy rose to her heart. This was different than when she had switched before. She was still here, but not here at the same time. She had never experienced this before. It was like another part had taken over, but she could still be present at the same time. *Maybe this is what Mary calls co-consciousness.*

"Are you doing okay today?" Angela had a slight look of concern on her face.

She must have noticed how weird I am right now! Cindy wanted to scream and run out of the coffee shop, but instead, she found herself responding calmly. "I'm fine. Sorry, just a little tired."

"I can understand that." Angela seemed to relax a little. "It sounds like life has been kind of challenging for you lately."

"I like the way you do that." Cindy gave a weak smile.

"Do what?"

"The way you make it seem like it is perfectly normal to live a messy life."

Angela gave a light laugh. "Life is messy. Sometimes more than others." She took a sip of her coffee. "So, how was your mom's birthday party?"

Suddenly, Cindy was swirling, dizzy, gone.

"What just happened?" Gabe asked. "She seemed to be doing fine, and now she is on auto-pilot again."

Michael shook his head. "Gabe, trauma is one of the most complicated things you will encounter, especially severe trauma like Cindy experienced. She is doing better." Michael glanced down at Cindy to make sure she was okay before continuing.

Cindy looked relaxed and was chatting about the cake and pastry puffs at the party.

Michael continued, "The slightest thing can cause Cindy to become overwhelmed. When that happens, she switches. She changes to one of her other identities. A part of herself that isn't overwhelmed."

"So then, how can you say she is doing better?"

"Simple, she was able to stay present longer this time before she became emotionally overwhelmed."

Gabe shook his head. "But in the last session, so much of the evil that was connected to her was severed; evicted by the Most High God! How can she still be struggling so much?"

"This isn't just a matter of spiritual warfare. This is a matter of the heart. Cindy's heart was broken. The intensity of the trauma split the essence of who she is into many, many parts. The Lord is healing these parts and knitting the different identities back together, but it takes time."

Cindy's laugh interrupted them for a moment. She was definitely on auto-pilot, saying and doing all of the "normal" things one might expect at coffee with the pastor's wife.

Gabe thought for a moment, "So, why doesn't the Lord just say the word and make her whole again?"

"He could, but then she would miss out on much." Michael gazed at Cindy, and Gabe sensed he had a deep regard for her and her journey. "She wouldn't develop properly, the way God designed development. She wouldn't mature. She wouldn't be equipped to live her life." Michael turned back to Gabe. "You see, the Most High God is perfect in all that He does. He created the human development process; therefore, that process is perfect. The Lord is giving her a do-over on that development process. He is allowing her to grow and mature as she heals and does warfare. The human development process takes time, but it is perfect. Why would God change something that is already perfectly designed?"

"I see." Gabe nodded with a new understanding of the God he served. "He wouldn't change a process that is already perfect. So, the human development process is interwoven with emotional healing and warfare. It takes time because it was designed this way, and God's design is perfect."

"Now you are getting it." Michael smiled. "I think you may be ready to rejoin Ronan. You can transfer back to him when we are done here."

Gabe agreed. The two sat and watched Cindy and Angela talk about the weather, the church, and a concert coming to town.

Angela's angelic warriors had seemed alert for the first part of the meeting, but now they were settled, just watching. *The warfare must be over since Cindy switched,* Michael thought. But he knew there would be a battle another day. There was something different about Angela. He had a feeling the Lord was going to use her in Cindy's journey in a unique way.

Gabe saw Michael and the others out to Cindy's vehicle. He was so curious as to what would happen next that he didn't want to leave. But orders were orders. In a flash, he had rejoined Ronan and the others in Mary's office.

Chapter 4

Mary's next client was just arriving and settling into the deep, soft couch.

"I don't know her," Gabe said to Ronan as he began to reorient back to his previous assignment. "Is she a new client?"

"No, her name is Maggie. She used to see Mary several years ago. She received full healing and integration of her dissociation, and she has been doing well until about a month ago when she had a car accident."

Ronan and Gabe nodded to the new group of angels who had just joined the room. They were assigned to Maggie. It was a small group of four angels. They were fully armed, but their swords were in their sheaths. Three sat near Maggie, and one stood by the door. A single worshipper joined in with the slow but joyful song wafting through the small office.

The next hour consisted of Maggie discussing her week with Mary. She had experienced an increase in depression and had a great deal of difficulty getting to work each day. Mary listened and inserted a few clarifying questions or caring responses here and there.

As the session was drawing to an end, Mary asked if she could pray over any attacks of the enemy sent to harass and debilitate Maggie. Maggie agreed.

As Mary began to pray, three small demons appeared around Maggie. Each had a thread connecting them to her mind and heart. They were startled to be seen by the heavenly angels in the room, but they did not pull away from their assignment.

Maggie began to weep as one of the demons started whispering in her ear.

"Father, I ask that You silence every voice that is not of You." One of Maggie's guarding angels reached for his sword, and the demon instantly silenced his whispers. "What were you thinking about just then, Maggie?"

"It's just too much. It's all too much." Quiet tears were streaming down her face. "Being whole is so different than what I thought it would be. It's too much."

"Being whole is very challenging. There are so many aspects of your daily life that you have never before had to face on your own, let alone going through a car accident. Your Trauma Coping System handled it all for you before. Now you are doing it alone, and that can feel really overwhelming."

"It does. There is no one to help me."

"Do you mind if I ask Jesus about that?"

"About what?" Maggie shot a curious look at Mary as she reached for a tissue to wipe her tears.

"About feeling alone and overwhelmed."

"Sure." Maggie's head dropped, and she closed her eyes.

The three demons sat on alert, waiting for the moment when they would be released to speak again.

Before Maggie's mind could wander too much, Mary began to pray, "Jesus, can You speak to Maggie about this loneliness she is feeling?"

Within a moment, a picture flashed into Maggie's mind. She could see herself sitting with Jesus in their special place. It was a beautiful meadow with tall trees on one side and a long mountain range on the other. There were blue and yellow flowers growing throughout the field, and she and Jesus were sitting on a large rock near the tree line. The sun felt warm on her face. She enjoyed the comfort of being here with Him.

As Maggie leaned into the picture, the demons cringed.

"They hate her faith, don't they?" Gabe stated it as more of a fact than a question.

"Yes, they do. As she leans into Jesus, they feel the heat of their destruction coming. But they are tied to her until her heart comes into agreement with Jesus, so they stay, but they are not comfortable!"

Gabe smiled. He enjoyed seeing the power of the Most High God at work!

"What is He saying?" Mary inquired.

Maggie waited a moment before responding. "It's really more of a sense," she paused again as if listening to something internal. "I have a deep sense that I am not alone. I have never been alone."

Tears began to stream down Maggie's face again.

"God has always been here for me." She continued with her focus on Jesus, "Then why can't I feel You, Lord? Why can't it always be like it is right now?"

Maggie paused again as Mary scribbled a few notes on her notepad.

"I don't really have words to describe what He is showing me," Maggie started. "It's like He is always here whether or not I feel Him, but as my faith grows, so does my awareness of Him. It's almost like my faith dissolves the layer of fog between earth and heaven."

Mary nodded in agreement with what Maggie was saying.

"Satan wants me to believe I am alone, so I will become overwhelmed and defeated, but Satan is a liar." Maggie's face softened a little as she said just under her breath, "I know the truth."

Maggie couldn't help but smile now, and a small chuckle came out of her mouth. "I do know the truth. God has always been there, and He is with me now."

The ties connecting Maggie to her persecutors began to loosen.

"I choose Your truth, Jesus. I reject the lies of the enemy."

That was all her angel needed. In one quick motion, the ties broke away from Maggie, and the angel's sword slashed through all three demons leaving only a vapor of black smoke, which faded into nothingness. She was free.

The angels by her side smiled. They had been waiting to do that for some time now.

Mary smiled too. Although she could not see what was happening in the spirit world, she could sense it.

"Does that feel better, Maggie?" Mary asked with a smile.

Maggie blew her nose and wiped her eyes again. She nodded "yes." Her sparkle was back, and Mary knew that her faith had been renewed.

After a wrap-up prayer, Mary told Maggie that she could spend some more time with Jesus in the prayer room if she were not ready to leave yet. Maggie thanked her but opted to head back home. "I have a new sense of purpose and things that need to get done!" she said with enthusiasm.

Mary smiled as Maggie left the room. Her angelic band followed her out—each nodding politely to Ronan and his troops as they went.

As Maggie drove home, she found herself humming softly and noticed her fingers tapping the steering wheel to the beat of her own song. She smiled and chuckled. It had been years since she felt this. She didn't even know what it was, but she liked it. She allowed herself to continue to hum. Throughout the rest of the day, Maggie was productive. She got her house clean and her bills paid. She even went to the grocery store and restocked her fridge. As bedtime approached, she went through her routine and snuggled under the blankets. She was still surrounded with a felt sense of the Lord's companionship. Maybe integration wasn't so bad after all.

Across town, Cindy was also sleeping soundly. But then, at 3 a.m., Cindy was startled and sat straight up in bed. She could feel her heart beating fast. Rabok was by her side, as usual, providing a safety net for rest. He could feel her anxiety rising as Salih moved in closer to help steady her emotions.

Michael was already on alert. He had sent Kaleb and Hezek around the perimeter of the house and down the hallway. Michael stood at the foot of her bed with his sword drawn. The room was full of sound, but nothing was visible. His face was steady. There was no fear in him but a simple resolve to protect Cindy.

Cindy rubbed her eyes and picked up her phone to check the time. She noticed a few texts had been sent to Mary. The first text, sent around midnight, read:

We know Jesus is still with us, but we cannot see Him anymore.

Cindy's heart sank, she didn't want to keep reading, but she did. At 2 a.m., she sent three more texts. One of those read:

We are scared. She is asleep. We know Jesus is here, but we still feel afraid. It is dark, but we are too scared to get out of bed to turn on the lights. We will hide under the blankets until it is safe.

Cindy was frozen in her bed. She hated that she had sent those texts. She didn't want to bother her therapist in the middle of the night. She wanted to be okay. She wanted to be at peace. Why wasn't she still at peace?

Dissociation is the worst thing that has ever happened to me! Worse than the trauma!

Her head began to swarm with thoughts of worry and confusion.

Why didn't what happened in session last longer?

I just want Jesus.

If I just didn't have these parts or self-images, or whatever they are!

Where is Jesus?

You are not good enough for Him to stick around!

I don't have to be. He loves me.

He loves everyone. There is nothing special about you.

I am broken; that's what's special about me.

Why can't I feel Him? Where is He?

I am alone.

As her mind pounded with questions and fears, she could feel anxiety rising from her stomach to her chest. It was all too much, too, too much.

Salih began to minister to her spirit.

She flung herself as deep into her bed as she could force her body to go and pulled the blankets up to cover her head.

Rabok tried to cover her with rest, but her thoughts were too fierce to interrupt.

Sleep, I just needed to sleep, just get away from everything, sleep...

That was enough permission to allow Rabok to provide a space of rest for her, but the battle was building around her.

Clank, slash, clink! Flashes of light and a flurry of swords flew throughout Cindy's home as she drifted off to sleep.

"Rabok and Salih, stay close to her while she sleeps," Michael commanded as he swung his heavy sword through two demons near the front window.

A huge black demon was fighting both Kaleb and Hezek in an attempt to get into the bedroom.

Suddenly, four warrior angels swooped into the room with their swords drawn. In that instant, all of their swords began to glow, and Michael knew someone was praying.

"You four stay around her bed," he instructed as he moved into position to help. "We cannot allow them to have contact with her."

Angels began taking their assignments while battling the demons trying to flood the room. A bright white light had settled over Cindy's bed as she slept. The contrast between the peace in the bedroom and the battle in the living room was intense.

"Where are they coming from?" a new warrior asked. His sword pierced through one demon and sent another, hurtling through the roof.

"Fear sent them," Michael shouted above the chaos.

The battle raged inside the home throughout the night while Cindy slept. She was protected by the ministering and warrior angels and surrounded by a warm, bright light.

When the sun rose over the small neighborhood houses, the noise in the house had finally begun to calm. Chaos, fear, and confusion had made strong efforts to retaliate against the healing work Jesus had done in Cindy's heart that week. They were unsuccessful. While Michael and his angels had stood firm and did not allow them to enter Cindy's bedroom, her sleep was still fitful and difficult. Parts of her did not believe she was safe. They were torn by the reality of their life experience and the truth Jesus was telling them about His presence with them. They needed help to make sense of it, to make sense of Him.

Across town, Mary was awake, phone in hand, interceding on Cindy's behalf.

Chapter 5

As the judge finished his instructions, many in the courtroom wondered whether or not a decision could be reached today, before the weekend, or would the victims have to wait until Monday. The jury filed out of the courtroom through a door behind the judge's desk and down a narrow hallway. Raphael and his troops were mingled throughout the jurors with his strongest warriors at the front and back of his group. There were plenty of unruly spirits wrestling to gain back control within the line of people headed into the deliberation room. Still, the attacks targeted from outside of the group were the greater battle.

As the jurors went one by one into the room where they would spend the next few hours, the evil attached to each of them was checked at the door. Generational curses, soul ties, and the bondage of sinful life were not allowed to participate. Mary had prayed before the jurors even left the courtroom that these spirits would not be allowed to be in the room during the deliberation. She could not do anything about their attachment to this group of twelve strangers, but she did have some authority to keep them from interfering.

Outside of the small deliberation room, spirits of chaos, lies, deception, and confusion were battling the angels stationed around the courthouse. Once all of the jurors were seated in the room, the angelic warriors lined the walls facing the twelve jurors, swords drawn and ready for battle. They could sense the evil battling their comrades just a few feet behind their backs, but they could also feel the presence of the Holy Spirit entering the room and settling in. His presence was much stronger than anything happening outside of the room, and with Him came a strong sense of truth and justice.

Raphael could sense the jurors relaxing a bit. The weight of the case was heavy on most of them, but the relief from their own spiritual baggage seemed to be having an impact. After a few awkward moments of gauging each other, a conversation began regarding the case.

"I have had some experience with all of this," started one of the jurors, a man in his forties dressed neatly in jeans and a polo. "I mean, this is my second time on a jury. I don't mind taking the lead unless someone else wants it?"

The jurors glanced at each other.

"How do we know who should be in charge?" a petite-sized woman with wide-rimmed glasses asked as she tugged on her collar, loosening it a bit from her skin.

"It doesn't really matter," another man stated gruffly. "Won't change my vote regardless of who's in charge."

After a few other jurors commented, the room fell quiet, and the initial juror took the lead. No one seemed to argue. "Should we vote first just to see where everyone stands, or does anyone have any questions?"

One by one, they went around the large table stating their vote and a summary of the belief behind their vote. As the discussion ensued, an occasional demon would make it through the outside forces and fly into the room like a ball of red lightning. Each time, they were met by a fiery blade from one of the warriors. After a while, it began to be a bit of a game among the warriors to see who could get the most.

Raphael smiled. He loved seeing the power of the Lord at work. He would occasionally listen in on the dialogue among the jurors. They took their job very seriously and worked through all of the details presented to them over the previous few days. The jury was split on their opinions, each juror weighing the evidence based on their own experience, reasoning, and personality tendencies.

"The things that man did were awful, simply awful," stated the petite woman with a shiver.

"We don't know he did anything," the gruff man retorted.

"The evidence sure seems to indicate he was guilty," a professional woman who had been mostly quiet up to that point added. "I mean, there were so many details..."

"Details can be made up; manufactured stories don't mean anything without evidence."

"How do you find evidence from thirty years ago?" a plumber in his thirties piped in from the far end of the table.

"He was careful, but that doesn't mean he isn't guilty." The petit woman was firm in her opinion.

The Holy Spirit was still present and strong. He was patient with the group, with their questions and their concerns. He even seemed pleased with the time they were taking to process the information. Raphael could see the Holy Spirit was not telling the jurors what to do. He was using each of their giftings together to explore the facts, uncover the deception and deceit, and discover truth...together. Seeing the analytical, empathic, strong-willed, quiet, and artistic thinkers all work together was actually quite beautiful. Without their individual spiritual entourages bringing chaos, whispering lies, and creating conflicts between their personality types, they were able to do something very holy with the gentle leading and revelation of the Holy Spirit.

"I can't imagine a man doing those things to his own family members." The petite woman now had tears welling in her eyes.

"Let's not be emotional about this." The lead juror was taking charge again. "We need to look at the facts of the case. We can't put a man in prison for the rest of his life unless we are very, very sure he did these things." He pushed his glasses up the bridge of his nose and waited for someone to respond.

Silence passed through the room.

Suddenly, three red demons flew through the ceiling. They were immediately beheaded by the two warriors closest to their entrance. "The battle must be increasing outside," noted Raphael, surprised to see three get through the outside forces at one time. "Benjamin, please go see how they are doing."

Benjamin saluted and flew through the wall and into the main lobby of the courtroom. A few people were sitting and waiting. A lady was typing on her computer, and several others were scrolling on their phones. He could hear the clanking of sword fight just outside the lobby doors. He gently passed through the room of oblivious people. It seemed the warriors outside of the deliberation room had pushed back the demonic attack to just outside the courtroom, but the war there was thick. There were at least a hundred angelic warriors stationed at every angle of the courthouse. Each was fighting a slew of demons with no end in sight. Their placement was strategic, and they were doing an honorable job keeping the demons from entering the building. Still, their forces seemed to be becoming more and more overrun by the minute.

Benjamin took a quick assessment of the type of attack they were under. He recognized the usual courthouse harassers: lies, confusion, chaos, shame, anger, and hate, but there were a few that were less common attacking from above. Two counterfeit cosmic beings, the spirits of universe and enlightenment, were stationed far above the building, strategically sending large groups of their troops to various points of the building that seemed weak or under-guarded. If they were there, the battle would only increase until a verdict could be found.

As Benjamin hurried back into the courthouse to make his report, a tall black demon shot down the hall and knocked Benjamin to the floor. Benjamin shook his head and looked up in time to see a sharp dagger plunging toward his head. In a flash, his sword was drawn and met the dagger inches in front of his face. The demon was strong. Neither flinched for a moment, but Benjamin could feel his strength building. The Lord distributed the prayers of the saints wherever needed in this battle, and he definitely needed that strength now.

In a moment, their positions were reversed. The black being was thrown off balance and found himself under the warrior of the Most High God. Before the demon could respond, Benjamin had thrust his sword through the middle of the being, and black vapor filled the air then dissipated. Benjamin paused for a moment to catch his breath, but before he could continue down the hall, a rowdy bunch of demons came from around the corner. Benjamin flew into action. He knocked two down with his sword, but another advanced from behind and took a swipe at his side.

Benjamin turned and rolled in the air toward the demon taking off his head and slicing through the side of another nearby. The two remaining demons flew by him and into the room full of jurors. Benjamin wasn't too worried about them. He knew the kind of greeting they would receive as they entered the room.

Benjamin followed but had to duck as he entered the room when one of the warriors almost took a strike at him too. They shared an apologetic nod, and then Benjamin headed to Raphael's position.

"The troops have pushed the enemy to the outside of the courthouse, but there are still a few getting into the building. Once inside, there is no one there to stop them."

"They must be fighting hard to have taken the battle outside." Raphael nodded in appreciation to the Most

High God for the strength in the battle. "Still," he continued, "we should station a few warriors to patrol the hallways to keep those who get by in line."

Benjamin agreed. "Also, there are two cosmic beings stationed far above the courthouse, the spirits of universe and enlightenment."

Raphael nodded slowly. "Are they interfering?"

"They are," Benjamin confirmed. "They are sending troops in by the dozens. They are carefully watching for the weaker areas and trying to sneak them by."

"So, this is not a regular attack."

"No, sir. It appears to be backed by these high-powered cosmic beings."

"Thank you, Benjamin."

Benjamin saluted as Raphael moved to a different position in the room. "I need to attend to the battle outside. Mechak, take the lead in here. The warriors are holding things down, but make sure they stay in formation and don't get too relaxed. Send three of our warriors to monitor the halls in the courthouse."

Mechak saluted. Raphael took one last look at the jurors and left the room. As he passed through the waiting room, he could see it was filling up. People were looking anxious and worrisome. The longer the jurors were deliberating, the more difficult it would be to keep the place clear of demonic interference. As Raphael approached the battle outside, he quickly scanned the area to find the lead warrior. Ronan was near the main entrance to the courthouse. He was simultaneously fighting a steady flow of demons and shouting orders to a group of warriors newly assigned to the courthouse.

Raphael drew his sword and approached Ronan's side.

"Do we have enough troops?" he shouted as his sword met the knife of a drooling spirit of rage.

"We are short on the north side," Ronan shouted back as he slashed his sword through the mid-section of two demons and engaged in a sword battle with another. "The troops on the roof seem to be holding their own, but I am not sure that will last. The cosmic beings are increasing their attacks in frequency and intensity."

Raphael slashed his sword through six approaching demons and engaged in a sword battle with a strong demonic entity who came from above. "Where is Mary?" he asked Ronan.

"Last I saw, she was in the witness room with her client."

"I will hold things down here. You should check on her."

Ronan nodded in agreement. He took one last stab with his sword through a harassing spirit and then darted into the building. Raphael didn't miss a beat. He moved into Ronan's spot and continued battling with fierce authority.

As Ronan moved through the courthouse, he fought a few demons who dared to approach, but mostly he left the interior battle to those assigned.

He dropped through the ceiling and settled into the witness room beside his charge, Mary. He enjoyed the flow of the Holy Spirit, which allowed him to easily move between a fierce battle and a calm and peaceful demeanor in a matter of seconds. While he wasn't engaged in sword battle in this room, he sensed the atmosphere was just as intense.

Mary was sitting with Cindy. Both were calm and quiet, but Ronan could sense the tension they were experiencing internally. When Cindy was called to be a witness against her uncle, she struggled to accept it. Of course, she didn't have much of a choice. You can't really ignore subpoenas. She had asked Mary to be with her, and Mary had agreed.

"This waiting is brutal," Cindy said with a weak smile.

"I know." Mary patted her hand. "The waiting and not knowing can be worse than having to testify."

"It is worse. I don't even remember testifying. I have no idea what I said on the stand." Cindy's voice trailed off, as did her eyes. "I remember seeing his face, my uncle, and I remember spelling my name for the court reporter. I think I spelled it wrong. That's all I remember."

"You did fine," Mary reassured her. "Your testimony was clear and concise. The rest is in the Lord's hands."

Ronan could feel Mary's faith as she silently said a prayer of peace for her client.

Cindy's uncle was not directly involved with Cindy's childhood abuse, but he was a terrible man. He had gone to jail just over a year ago when it was discovered he had been abusing his two daughters. His trial was this week, and Cindy was asked to testify on behalf of her cousins. They had told her things about the abuse that they had not told anyone else.

"What do you think will happen?" Cindy inquired.

"I honestly have no idea." Mary looked past Cindy and out the window as she talked. "I'd like to believe the verdict will come back guilty, and he will get life in prison, but it is so hard to tell with cases like this."

"But the things he did. He was...it was so awful. How could he not get convicted?"

The pain in Cindy's eyes tore at Ronan's being. He knew the choices her uncle had made grieved the Lord deeply. The uncle had hurt more children than would ever be known in this courthouse, and Ronan wanted him to be found guilty as well. But Mary was right. This case could go either way.

"I'm just not sure how the jury will interpret the evidence that was presented."

"I sure wish I could be a fly in that room right now to know what they are saying."

Mary nodded in agreement, and the two were silent again.

Things seemed to be handled here. It was time Ronan get back to the battle. He silently asked the Lord to keep the battle fresh in Mary's mind. He saw her set her hand on her Bible as he left the room, and he knew she would be praying.

The battle outside was intensifying. Ronan took his position back from Raphael without exchanging words, and Raphael headed back to the deliberation room to get an update.

"So, we are in agreement?" the lead juror asked as he jotted a note on his tablet.

They had been deliberating for the entire day at this point. Their tiredness could be felt in the air.

"I'm still not sure." The petite woman shook her head. "What if we are wrong?"

"Ugh, let's get this done already." The gruff man sat with his arms crossed, barely tolerating the process.

"I'm calling for a vote."

One by one, they went around the table and gave their vote. It was unanimous.

"Finally, now at least I can make it home for dinner." The gruff man stood and pushed his chair in with a huff.

The lead juror called in the guard and told him they were ready.

Within fifteen minutes, they were all seated back in the courtroom, waiting for the judge to pronounce the verdict.

Mary and Cindy sat at the back of the courtroom. Cindy had her eyes pinched shut, and Mary was loosely holding her hand.

The spiritual battle in and around the courtroom was lessening as all were waiting to hear the final verdict.

"Do you have a verdict?" the judge asked the jury.

"We do," the lead juror responded. "We find James Colmain not guilty on all counts."

The courtroom burst open with wails and cheers alike. The uncle's wife was visibly relieved and embraced James with relief in her eyes. The victims, who were now young adults, and the prosecution witnesses were grieved and crying. Some held hands and embraced, some sat in silence with tears streaming down their faces, others were motionless, trying to allow the news to sink in.

The jury left the courtroom first, then the uncle, his wife, and other supporters were escorted out next. The rest were requested to wait in the courtroom until the freed abuser had left the property.

"The pain in this room is unbearable," Benjamin muttered.

"It is," Raphael responded. "The pain in heaven right now is even deeper."

"How could this happen?" one of the angelic warriors asked. "The presence of the Holy Spirit was so strong in the deliberation room. How could they get it so wrong?"

The battle had all but ended now. A few warriors fought off spirits of rage and torment who were harassing those left in the courtroom.

"Every man and woman on that jury had a choice to make," Raphael began. "We can keep Satan from interfering, and we can bring clarity to their minds, but we cannot decide for them." He thought for a moment before he continued, "Each juror uses their knowledge and experience to filter the information presented to them during the trial and to make a decision."

"I doubt any of the jurors have ever had experience with this level of evil," Ronan added. "It is deep, dark, and manipulative. They couldn't see through the trick, and there was not enough evidence presented to help them make a better decision."

The angels were silent, leaving only the sounds of soft cries and angry whispers throughout the room.

The doors opened, and a bailiff entered. "You may leave now."

Cindy had been quiet since the verdict had been read. As she and Mary left the building, she finally found a few words.

"Where was the justice?"

"Justice?" Mary responded.

"Yes, my cousins will never have justice now. What about them? What will they do? How can they live with this?" Tears were filling her eyes, but she refused to run.

Mary stopped and turned to face Cindy.

"Cindy, this is very important." She waited until Cindy was able to focus on her face. "You have to know that God is the true Judge. He will always issue justice, regardless of what man does."

Angels of peace began surrounding the two ladies standing on the sidewalk outside the courtroom. Cindy's shoulders began to relax.

"But it seems so unfair to wait until heaven for justice." Cindy wiped a tear that had finally made its way down her face.

"God does have timing in all He does, but justice begins here on earth. Justice happens in ways we will never know, but it does happen."

"I don't understand. I may never understand. I want to trust God; I just don't know if I can." Tears were released to stream down Cindy's face.

Mary handed Cindy a tissue from her purse. "It's a lot to process." She waited while Cindy blew her nose. "I think the best thing you can do now is to get some rest. God will help you understand in His time."

Cindy nodded in agreement.

"Remember, we scheduled an extra session on Monday to help you process all that happened this week." Mary paused as she pulled another tissue from her purse for Cindy. "God will get you through this."

Cindy wiped her tears and gave Mary a weak smiled. Mary returned the smile and gave Cindy a brief hug before the two headed to their cars. Cindy knew the weekend would be difficult, but she also trusted the Lord would see her through.

Mary followed as Cindy began walking toward her car. So did Rabok, Salih, and the rest of the troop of ministering angels that had been assigned to them for the day.

Chapter 6

Monday morning, Mary started work early. There was much to do. She had no idea what the Lord had in store, but she knew it would be special. Three morning clients came and went. Ronan, Gabe, and the others stood by watching the Holy Spirit work through Mary in different and powerful ways with each person. There were a few more battles throughout the afternoon, but mostly she just showed love and patience to each client and then connected them to a member of the Holy Trinity for deep healing and strength.

As the workday came to an end, Ronan could sense the Holy Spirit refreshing Mary for her last session.

"It has been quite the day," Gabe commented.

"Yes, it has. The Lord has been glorified all day long in this office." Ronan looked toward the door. "And now He will be glorified even more."

Cindy entered the room with her angelic band of warriors and ministering angels.

"Hi, Cindy." Mary brushed her hair back from the side of her face as she looked up from her desk. "Have a seat."

Cindy moved into her usual spot on the couch. The cushions seemed to sink a little lower than usual, but she didn't mind. Mary transitioned from behind her desk into the comfy chair adjacent to the green couch. Cindy just stared blankly at the floor while Mary adjusted her glasses and notepad.

"So, how have you been sleeping? I know the trial on Friday was really hard on you. It was hard on everyone."

Cindy thought for a moment. "It was okay. I mean, I really don't even remember much since Friday." She fidgeted with her hair. "What happened? I mean, I remember being at the courthouse, at least a little. I remember the jury said..." Her eyes began to water. "I remember the jury didn't get it right." Her face dropped slightly. "I don't remember much after that."

"Well, we waited in the courtroom for a little while. Then we walked out to the car together. After we got a bite to eat, I dropped you off at home."

"Oh, I forgot about that." Cindy searched the room with her eyes looking for her next words. "I just don't understand. I don't understand any of this."

Mary waited patiently, giving Cindy the time she needed to process the thoughts that had undoubtedly been swirling around her mind, hidden behind walls of denial and pain.

"I mean, how can a good God let this happen?" Her left hand was tracing the pattern on the couch as she talked. "I mean, He let the abuse happen to begin with, and now this?"

Mary could tell Cindy was trying to be calm and rational, but she knew that Cindy needed to access the emotion locked away inside. So, she waited.

Cindy didn't seem to notice the lull in the conversation. She continued to trace the pattern on the couch.

Mary quietly prayed for the Lord to release holy empathy into the room that would allow Cindy the safety to feel her own heart. Salih moved in closer to Cindy. The Holy Spirit began to fill the space between Salih and Cindy.

Slowly, Cindy's hand stopped moving, and tears began to slide down her face.

"I'm so sorry, Cindy," Mary started once she could sense Cindy's heart in the room. "I'm so very sorry."

Cindy covered her face with both hands and sobbed. A low, child-like cry came from deep in her heart. Everyone in the room knew this was about more than just her uncle and her cousins. This was about all of the injustice she faced in her own life: the misery, the abuse, the lack of closure, and healing. She cried harder and deeper for a few moments, and then the tears shut off.

"It's good to cry. There is a lot of pain stored up inside." Mary waited for Cindy to respond.

"I know. I don't like to let it out." Cindy took a tissue from the small table next to the couch and blew her nose.

"Let's ask the Lord to join us. Would that be okay with you?"

"I don't know. I know the right answer is 'yes,' but I'm just not sure He wants to see me right now."

"Why is that?"

"Because. What I have inside right now is not good."

"What is inside, Cindy?"

"I don't want to say. It's too bad. It's wrong. I shouldn't feel this way." Cindy's face was hardening. Any trace of the tears from just a few moments ago was gone.

"It's okay. Whatever you have to say. It is safe to say here."

Cindy's eyes narrowed as she studied Mary's face for a moment.

"I'm angry." Her tone was harsh, and her fist was wrapped tightly around her Kleenex. "I'm angry at the uncle. I'm angry at my parents. I'm angry at God." She stared at Mary, almost defying her to respond, ready to fight and argue with whatever Mary might say.

Mary was quiet for a moment. Salih was still giving the Holy Spirit space to allow Cindy to feel her heart, feel the anger, the intense emotions buried so deep she was rarely able to feel them, let alone say the words aloud. It was a live miracle happening right there in the small office.

Mary spoke in a gentle, quiet voice, "I'm so glad."

Cindy's face relaxed slightly. "Of course you are," she retorted.

"Feeling this anger is so important for you, Cindy. It's been buried inside for so long."

"Well, I am angry, and I am not going to apologize for it." Words were forming in Cindy's mind to express the anger she had never been able to express before. "They don't deserve forgiveness. I know that's what you're going to say, but they don't deserve it! They are evil, pure evil! There is no excuse for how they treated us, how they treated me!" Salih sat peacefully next to her, providing her with the peace and safety to allow the anger to ooze from her being. Ronan smiled. This was a big achievement for Cindy.

"So, tell me why." Cindy leaned forward, daring Mary to answer. "Why did God just leave me like that? Why did He just let it happen? Why did He let that evil man get out of jail yesterday? Humph, God didn't even show up to court!" She plopped back on the couch with her arms crossed. She looked more like an angry teenager than the grown woman she was.

"You have every reason to be angry." Mary sat, waiting for Cindy to say more.

Cindy had reached her limit of how much anger she would allow herself to express. Her demeanor changed as she switched out of her personality's angry part and into a part that carried much guilt and shame.

As her shoulders slumped, she covered her eyes with both hands. "I'm sorry; I know I should have never said those awful things!" Her voice was weak and shaky. "I'm so, so sorry!" She was crying again, but for a different reason.

She blew her nose with the partially used Kleenex still in her hand.

Salih was still at work, allowing empathy to flow from the Holy Spirit into the space around the couch. Rabok joined him, giving Cindy's physical body rest from the intense expression of emotion she just had.

"It is so beautiful to see the healing process flow," Gabe commented.

"It is," Ronan agreed. "A part of God's perfect design."

Mary leaned forward. This was where the work needed to be done. "Cindy, there is no shame in being angry. Your anger is righteous. It is holy."

"How can you say that!" Cindy replied, horrified at the thought. "No, no, no! My anger is wrong! It is a sin!"

Cindy was now switching back and forth between anger over the abuse and shame over the anger.

"Lord God, I take authority over the spirit of shame, and I ask that You silence every voice that is not of You."

At Mary's request, Ronan slid his sword through a tormenting spirit of shame that appeared hovering nearby, and two large angels shoved a man-sized demon against the wall, covering his mouth with their powerful hands.

"Now, Cindy, is that a little better?"

Cindy nodded. It was quiet now except for the steady hum of Aria and Rani worshipping the Lord near the doorway.

"I still feel like this anger is wrong. I don't know how to change that." She was calm and feeling her heart again.

"We are at the root of her conflict with anger and injustice now," Ronan said, nodding with approval toward his band of angels spread throughout the room.

Mary took her glasses off and laid them on the table as she closed her eyes in prayer. "Let's ask the Lord about it."

Cindy nodded as she bowed her head as well.

Mary began the courtroom prayer, and Ronan's charges moved into their courtroom positions.

"Wait." Cindy's head tilted to the left for a moment.

Mary waited.

"The Lord is speaking to her," Ronan said to no one in particular.

"You know what I just realized?" Cindy's eyes were wide open, now staring at Mary with awe.

"What's that?"

"I just realized that God always gives good results when we go to His courtroom! He never fails. His verdicts are always right, and He issues punishments right away!" A smile was starting to creep onto Cindy's face.

"That's true," Mary affirmed, "in the courtroom of the Most High God, justice always prevails. God uses man's courtroom to issue justice on earth when possible, but man is not perfect, so man's courtroom will never be perfect. God, however..."

Cindy interrupted Mary with excitement. "God is perfect! So, this is where He issues justice."

Peace washed over Cindy as she sunk into the couch. A thousand tons lifted from her shoulders.

The fierce demon who had been restrained against the wall gave one last growl and shove as he disappeared in a puff of smoke. "That will be the last we see of him." Ronan smiled. "As people receive the truth of the Lord in their hearts, demons lose their influence."

"It's a beautiful sight!" Gabe was smiling as well.

"You are right, Cindy. Do you want to see what kind of justice God will be issuing today?"

Cindy nodded and closed her eyes again.

"Lord God, you are the Judge Over All Things. Where would you like to issue justice for Cindy today?" Mary waited.

Cindy could see the heavenly courtroom in her mind's eye. "I see a tall being. He is all black, and he is coated with something, something gross, like tar or oil. His smile is..." Cindy cringed and shivered. She didn't have the words.

Ronan and his troops could see the open portal in the room. The cosmic being, who had walked into the courtroom, was the spirit of shame. "He always coats people with shame and disgust and then forces them to look in his twisted mirror. As they look, they only see what he wants them to see, but they believe it is true."

"Evil doesn't play fair," Gabe noted.

"Evil doesn't, but the Most High God is fair and just."

"God, what do you want us to know about this being?" Mary asked the Judge.

Again, the Lord detailed all that this being had come from—the permissions given by Cindy's ancestors to invite him into the bloodline and the rituals and agreements made to keep him in full power.

Cindy's eyes were still closed as she winced. "The stories are so painful to hear."

"I know they are. Evil is a terrible thing. Shame is a terrible thing, but it's time to get rid of this today."

"But how? Those things he said…" Cindy searched for the words. "They were terrible, but they were true!" Her head was swimming with thoughts of all that was said. "Some of those things I even brought on myself. It wasn't anyone else's fault but my own. How can I ever be free from that?"

With her head in her hands, Mary could see tears running down Cindy's face. Mary moved over to the couch and sat next to her.

"Cindy," Mary started slowly, "this is one of those miracles of grace." She waited for Cindy to indicate she was listening. "You see, when Jesus died in the cross, he took all of the shame for us. He took the shame and punishment for every sin that you and your ancestors committed."

Cindy looked up with her hands still close to her face. Her eyes were red, but Mary knew she was listening.

Aria and Rani had shifted from a soft hum to a gentle melody of gratitude and praise.

Ronan looked around the room and saw each of the swords began to glow ever so slightly. The presence of the Holy Spirit was beginning to fill the room with the glory of the power of the resurrection of Christ.

With Cindy's permission, Mary placed her hand on Cindy's hand. "We are here, before the Lord, to do this together. You are not alone."

Cindy stared into Mary's eyes for a moment and then nodded her agreement. She closed her eyes once again and waited.

Ronan's troops stood ready for the clean-up after the Judge stated the verdict.

Mary began to pray.

"Cindy, do you forgive your ancestors for allowing this shame into the bloodline?"

"I do."

"Do you forgive your family for allowing it to grow in your heart and mind?"

"I do."

Mary continued the prayer, revoking and renouncing all permissions that the spirit of shame caused to be connected to Cindy. There was a steady increase in demonic activity filling the courtroom. Demons that had been attached to the spirit of shame in various ways were being pulled into the courtroom by the Most High God to stand judgment and hear the ruling with the rest of them.

"Most High God, I thank You that the death of resurrection of Jesus Christ covers any penalty or consequence for breaking these agreements with shame. The price He paid on the cross was more than enough to cover any debt owed here."

Mary ended her prayer, and there was a holy hush in the room. Even Aria and Rani were quiet now, but the vibration of worship could be felt emanating from the core of their being.

The spirit of shame fumed at what was prayed, but he said nothing.

Cindy's eyes were still closed. "The Lord says there is something else He wants me to know before He makes His ruling." Cindy sat, unsure of what the Lord might say. "He says the spirit of death that He ruled against a few sessions ago had to be gone before shame could be dealt with. They were connected. Death was keeping Shame in place. Just like when Jesus died on the cross. When death was defeated, there was no more shame for believers."

Mary nodded in agreement and silently thanked the Lord for the revelation to Cindy's heart.

"He is ready now." Cindy squeezed Mary's hand.

As the Lord revoked the permissions given to the spirit of shame over the decades, the demons surrounding Cindy and filling the courtroom began to swirl and run and scream. Ronan blocked Cindy's spiritual ears so she could not hear the flurry in the courtroom. Then, he and all of the warriors present made a quick end to each of the evil spirits attached to this being of shame.

"I see all of the evil swirling into the portal. The spirit of shame is being escorted out of the courtroom."

A large heavenly bailiff sent the spirit, with all of his underlings, into the portal with a final shove.

"The courtroom is clear, and the portal is closing." Cindy released her grip on Mary's hand. "I can see the Judge. He is smiling."

Cindy and Mary smiled as well.

"He wants to tell me something." A young version of Cindy was in the courtroom. She climbed up on the lap of the Judge. She was small, not just in size, but in age—a part of Cindy representing her past, maybe three years old. She was representing Cindy's entire system. She was cute but looked tired and worn.

"He is telling me how much He loves me, how He has always loved me. I feel so safe in His lap."

Cindy sat with the Lord for a few more moments while Mary transitioned back into her chair, patiently waiting for the Lord to complete His work in Cindy's heart.

Ronan and Michael and their angelic bands returned to their usual positions in the room now that the courtroom was empty.

"Wow, I don't know what to say." Cindy thought for a moment. "God is so good."

"Yes, He is." Mary was smiling. "What did He tell you?"

"He told me how important I was to Him. He loves me so much! I had no idea. I didn't realize how much shame was keeping me from His heart. He was always there for me, but I wouldn't let myself get near His heart because of the shame I felt about myself."

"That's a pretty big revelation."

"It is." Cindy paused. "And you know what else?" she continued without waiting for a response, "I think I can finally set boundaries with my parents."

"Really? What changed?"

"Well, I realized something. Just like shame was keeping me from my heavenly Father, shame was connecting me to my earthly father."

"How so?"

"Well, I know my dad is evil—at least part of me does—but I think I believed I deserved the evil. I deserved to be with him and my mom. I believed I wasn't good enough to be loved by anyone, so I had to stay with them." Cindy looked around the room as if searching for something. "I always thought the trauma was my enemy. This whole time I have been on this healing journey, I blamed the trauma, the abuse, and the pain for what it did to me. It made me shameful and dirty. I thought I either deserved it or wasn't strong enough to fight it off."

"I see. And now?" Mary inquired.

"Now, well, now it's all different." Cindy was searching for words again. "I know the trauma is not my enemy. It is what happened, but it is over now. It wasn't about me. The trauma was not my shame; the trauma was my parents' shame. Now that the shame is gone, I can receive love. I can receive forgiveness. I can be with others. I don't need my parents anymore." Cindy looked more relieved than happy. "And I am not like them." That last statement had a ring of finality to it.

The Holy Spirit had sent a tall, wise angel of clarity to sit with Cindy. The presence of this special gift allowed Cindy to see the truth in a way that was never possible before.

"So, what would you like to do?" Mary asked.

"I want to be free of them, free of my parents. I want to say "no" to them. I don't want to have to see them or speak to them ever again."

"Let's see if we can make that happen." Mary smiled at Cindy before closing her eyes to pray.

The two of them prayed a special prayer over Cindy's heart and mind, separating her from her parent's influence spiritually and emotionally. "This prayer will help you begin to set boundaries in a new way, Cindy."

Cindy nodded. A few tears were running down her face now, and she could feel the conflict inside about the decision. Salih began to intercede on her behalf, keeping the conflict close to the surface. "I still have parts who want to be with my parents. I think they are younger parts."

"I know." Mary looked at Cindy with soft eyes. "These little ones have always wanted a family. They want to be heard, and loved, and cared for. They have always imagined this with your parents, and they don't think they will survive if they give up on that dream."

A knot was forming in Cindy's throat. She confirmed Mary's statement with a nod as the tears continued to run.

"It's okay. These parts are important too."

Cindy dropped her gaze to the floor. The feelings were overwhelming.

Aria and Rani began to enter into a chorus of honor and respect to the Most High God.

"God is honored as Cindy honors herself in setting these boundaries," Michael commented. "It won't be easy, but it shows that she is beginning to value herself the way He does."

"Fascinating." Gabe was beginning to see God and His Creation in an entirely different light.

Mary pulled a special notebook from one of her bookcases. "Let's work on some practical boundaries together and see if we can find a way to honor your need for boundaries and your parts' need for family."

Cindy was now holding the box of Kleenex. With her knees pulled up to her chest, she gave a quick nod and wiped her eyes.

Mary and Cindy began outlining a list of boundaries to keep her safe from her family while trying to honor the needs of the other parts inside. When they were done, the list included:

- Deleting her parents on social media,
- Blocking their phone number from calling or messaging,
- Creating a list of responses that Cindy could use if they asked her to come over for any reason,
- Doing self-talk with the parts about what a healthy family looks like, and
- Finding a small group or a friend that she could spend some time with to help meet her need for family.

As they made the list, Ronan, Michael, and the others watched with great hope that Cindy would finally be free from the grip of her parents. An occasional demon would appear, whispering lies and doubts into Cindy's ears. Each time it was met with the same fate: death by sword.

When Cindy left the session that day, she had renewed hope. She would finally be free. She didn't know it, but the angels assigned to her were also celebrating the great victory of shame's defeat that happened in the courtroom of the Most High God! The rest of the day was uneventful, though Cindy was exhausted by the evening.

Around 8 p.m., she drank a hot cup of tea and then headed to bed. She wanted to read her Bible first, but she was too worried she might be triggered by something she read. She really wanted to keep the peace she was feeling as long as possible.

Chapter 7

The phone rang, waking Cindy with a start.

She reached for her cell phone from beside the bed while rubbing the sleep out of her eyes.

Ten a.m.? Wow, I had no idea I have been asleep so long!

She sat up and waited for her vision to clear so she could see who called.

Mom? My mom called?

Mom never calls!

Why did she call?

Does she know what happened in session yesterday?

That's stupid. How could she possibly know that!

She knows! She knows everything!

I am going to be in so much trouble!

A few demons appeared in the room near Cindy. Hezek sliced through them just in time to see the swarm of demons that were circling her mind.

Calm down, calm down. Think. Why would she be calling?

"A portal is open near the nightstand," Michael pointed, and Kaleb and Hezek moved in.

"How did it open?" Kaleb asked as he stabbed through demons trying to get around him.

"The Lord will show us," Michael responded as he gave direction to the other angels now joining them in the fight.

Cindy was pacing in her room now.

There has to be a reason! Why today, of all days?

I thought we took care of this yesterday? Didn't God say He would protect me?

As I thought, you can't trust Him.

Of course, we can trust Him! We have to trust Him!

We did trust Him, and look what happened!

The demons were not quite filling the room, but there was a steady stream coming through the portal now. The warriors were fighting, but they were greatly outnumbered.

"Worry and fear are adding to the bunch," Michael stated, a little out of breath. "They must have been given permission to be here somehow."

"We aren't even slowing them down!" Kaleb seemed worried.

"Just keep battling those that come through. The Lord will show us what to do."

Just then, Cindy noticed a few new text messages on her phone.

"Oh no," she whined. "Why, oh why!"

Michael glanced over her shoulder while sparing with two demons at once. "That is how they got permission," he said just above a whisper. He then ordered Rabok and Salih to Cindy's side as he continued to battle the demons coming through the portal. He turned to Kaleb and Hezek, who were still battling at the portal opening. "While she was texting Mary last night, a part sent a text to her mom at 2 a.m., asking if she could come home."

"Why did she do that?" Kaleb was in disbelief.

Slash! A handful of demons met their demise just as they entered the room.

"Well, it wasn't purely her; it was a part of her. She must have switched to a younger part and sent the text while the others were texting Mary," Michael explained as best he could, given the commotion in the room.

The hissing and sneering were getting loud, and the room was getting dark.

"We need this portal closed!"

Just then, a band of angelic reinforcements darted into the room. Michael recognized them; they had been called in to help with his charges before. "Samson, Jason, focus on the panic around her head. Samuel and Peyton, protect the ministering angels so they can help bring her into a sound mind. She knows how to deal with this. We just have to give her the space to remember." Michael took a quick assessment of the room. "The rest of you create two tiers, one to spear anything that comes through the portal and a second-tier to get the demons that get by the first tier."

The angelic troops moved like a fluid army flowing in sync with their commanding officer, and the battle continued getting darker and more intense by the minute.

Cindy was frantic now as her mind whirled with fear and shame. "You know how to handle this, Cindy, think!" Self-talk wasn't working fast enough, and Cindy could feel herself sinking, sinking, sinking...

She shifted into another part. This part didn't feel much. She was an adult part and generally calm and level-headed. She sent a text to Mary:

A little part texted mom. Mom just called.

> Darkness is overtaking me. We know Jesus is
> still with us, but we cannot see Him anymore.

She waited. No response.

Space began to clear between the ministering angels and Cindy's mind. The warriors were holding their own with the evil entities flooding the room. Their swords began to glow.

"Someone is praying," Michael observed.

"Who?"

"I'm not sure, but their prayers are reaching the Lord, and we are gaining strength."

Cindy sat on the edge of her bed with her head in her hands.

Okay, you can do this.

No, you can't. You couldn't stop the evil then, and you can't stop it now.

God can stop it. God will stop it. I just have to. I have to...

Cindy closed her eyes and whispered a prayer, "Lord, please help me."

That was all it took. The Holy Spirit accepted the invitation to help and settled into the quickly clearing space between the ministering angels and Cindy. He whispered truth into her spirit.

"I know!" Cindy closed her eyes again. "Permission, I have to take back any permission I gave for this door to be opened!" Her head began to calm, but her voice was still shaky. "Lord, please forgive me for texting my mom. I really want to honor the boundaries Mary and I set yesterday. Please help me to honor those boundaries and remove anything of an evil spiritual nature that I may have opened the door to with my text."

Before the demons in the room knew what was happening, the portal was sucked away into a puff of smoke. There was nothing left to do but clean up the now homeless and directionless demons swarming around the room, desperate for a way of escape.

Michael's warriors made quick work of it, and in a few moments, the room was clear.

"Warriors, circle the perimeter to make sure we got them all. Rabok and Salih, stay by Cindy while she recovers."

Again, the angels followed orders with ease, rounding up the remaining darkness and ensuring Cindy had the space she needed to hear from the Holy Spirit.

Never mind. God helped.

Cindy pressed "send," letting Mary know the emergency was over. She wanted to go back to sleep, but she was far too awake. She sat up straight and went to stand. Her head swooshed, and she plopped back down.

Oh, too dizzy.

She put her head back in her hands for a moment and then tried again.

She shuffled her feet holding the wall while she made her way to the kitchen. The coffee was already brewed but cold.

Wow, I really did oversleep.

Why didn't I set the alarm?

I am so tired. I need to sleep to get better.

No, you are just lazy.

Clearly, her parts were awake.

She warmed up a cup of coffee in the microwave and sat at the little kitchen table by the window. It looked like a beautiful day. She pulled her feet up on the chair and wrapped her arms around her knees. Her coffee smelled good. She could feel her pounding heart began to slow its beat. Maybe this day was going to be okay.

The Holy Spirit was still present, close to Cindy. Salih kept the space open around Cindy's heart and mind for the Holy Spirit to work freely. The angelic band had dispelled the evil in the house, and the light of the Lord was flowing through the home.

"Things are good for now." Michael glanced around the house. "But stay on alert. I anticipate another battle coming." The additional troops stayed nearby in case they were needed.

Cindy took another sip of her coffee. As she sat her cup on the table, she absentmindedly picked up her phone and began flipping it over and over in her hand. As she stared out the window, she noticed a bluebird sitting on the fence in the neighbor's yard. It seemed so carefree. There was not a worry on its mind.

After a few minutes, the bird hopped to the ground, picked up some grass, and flew away. Cindy was reminded of the Bible verse in Matthew that says, "If God looks after the birds, how much more does He look after His children." She was His child.

"I am His," she said out loud.

The words felt foreign but true.

I am His.

She could feel the truth sinking into her heart.

Without thinking, she dialed her Pastor's wife.

"Hello?" the voice on the other end of the phone was kind and gentle.

"Hi. Um... is this Angela?"

"Yes, it is."

"Hi Angela, this is... um... this is Cindy, from church."

"Hi, Cindy! How are you doing?"

Angela seemed genuinely happy to hear from Cindy. Cindy wasn't sure what to do with that. She wasn't used to people being happy to hear from her. She wasn't even sure why she had called.

"Um... I'm not sure, really?"

"Are you okay?" Angela sounded concerned.

"Oh, yes, actually. I am good. I just called you. I'm not sure why."

"Well, I am headed out to run a few errands. Would you like to meet for coffee again? I have an hour or so later this morning."

"Um... well, okay." Cindy thought a moment. "Yes, actually, I would like that."

"Okay, then, I will see you at our spot around 11:30 a.m."

"Okay, see you then."

Cindy hung up. It felt good to be wanted.

Our spot? What's that about?

She was faking. She has to be nice to everyone. It's her job.

No, she wasn't faking.

Don't be so childish.

Cindy shook her head.

She got up and headed into her room to change. She was feeling good, and she wasn't going to let her parts ruin that for her.

She pulled a clean pair of jeans out of her drawers and began flipping through hangers in her closet to find a nice shirt. She wanted one to match her mood.

As she hunted through clothes that she hadn't looked at in months, the Holy Spirit eased back. She had received all of the grace needed for now. Rabok and Salih took their usual post nearby. The need for intense ministry had passed, and Cindy was in a good place now. Her spiritual entourage would be nearby should the need arise, and, of course, the Holy Trinity was always with her, but the battle was over for the moment.

She pulled a bright blue polo over her head and buttoned her jeans. They fit well. As she tied her tennis shoes, she tried to remember the last time she felt so much peace. She couldn't remember when that was. She took one last look in the mirror, content with what she saw, and she headed out the door with her purse and keys in hand.

The drive to the coffee shop was smooth and uneventful. Worship music played on the local radio station, and she drummed her thumb on the steering wheel to the beat of the song. As she parked the car outside the little coffee shop, she thought through the events of the day.

Michael took advantage of the moment to give instructions to his troops. "Check the inside to make sure it is clear. Jason and Samson, do a perimeter check. The rest of you, stay nearby and keep an eye on Cindy."

As the angels dispatched to their positions, Cindy said a prayer, "Father God, I know You have already done so much for me. I don't want to be greedy and keep asking for things, but I would really like to have someone to talk to. Could You please help this meeting to go well?"

"Simple, but effective," said Michael as he issued Salih to join Angela's angelic guard in the coffee shop. Salih knew the emotions Cindy needed to express to feel connected to Angela. He could coach Angela's group through the process.

Cindy exited the car and headed into the coffee shop.

Weird, I haven't switched much today.

Don't worry. We are all still here.

I don't know if that's good or bad.

I want to tell her.

Don't tell her anything! I mean it!

Just stop. I want to enjoy this.

Cindy ran her hand through her hair and waved her hand dismissively at her parts. With a shake of her head, she approached the table, ready for whatever might happen.

"Hi, Cindy! I'm so glad you could make it!" Angela stood up and hugged Cindy.

I'll never get used to this. Hugging is so not my thing.

"Hi!" Cindy greeted her back and leaned into the hug a bit just to spite the part inside.

"Can I get you a coffee or tea?"

"I'm fine." Cindy smiled as she sat down.

The coffee shop was pleasant. Cindy hadn't noticed the décor before. It was floral and rustic, with a big stone fireplace in the center. Tables were scattered around the room, giving each party ample room to talk and have some privacy. The waitress was friendly and brought Cindy and Angela water as they talked.

"So, what are you up to today?"

Cindy didn't know how to answer. "It's been a strange kind of day," she started.

"Would you like to talk about it?"

Don't you dare!

We need her! We can do this!

Mary said we need a friend. Angela seems nice.

She can't be your friend, stupid. She is your pastor's wife. She would never have a friend like you.

Stop it!

Michael noticed a demon approaching—Confusion. He could sense it. With a wave of his finger, he motioned to the closest warrior, who quickly stabbed the demon through the middle. He dissipated in a puff of smoke.

Cindy took a deep breath and let it out slowly. "Well, I guess it kind of started with therapy yesterday."

Angela nodded as she took a sip of her water. Her eyes were full of care and light that made Cindy feel safe enough to continue. As she talked, Salih, the angel on assignment to be with Angela's angelic band, shared his gift of supernatural empathy to the group. He was creating the space for Angela to allow the Holy Spirit to move deeply in her heart and mind.

Cindy continued, "You see, I have been trying to set some boundaries with my parents for months now." She shifted in her chair and took a drink of water. "I didn't know I needed to do that until recently. I know this may sound strong, but they are really toxic to me." She paused to see how Angela would handle such a strong word. Angela knew nothing about the horrors of Cindy's childhood, and Cindy was worried she would not understand.

Angela nodded. "It's wise to have good boundaries. Everyone should."

Cindy's face lit up.

Is this what acceptance feels like?

Don't get your hopes up.

"Yes, that's what my therapist tells me." Cindy gave a wry smile. "Anyway, I realized yesterday in counseling that shame had been holding me back. God healed me of shame, and things have been, well, things have been different since then."

"Things always change when God is working!" Angela smiled.

Cindy's water glass was empty, and Angela flagged down the waitress for more water.

"So, how is life different for you today?"

It's like she really wants to know!

What else is she supposed to say? She is just making small talk.

I don't believe that. I feel safe here. That must be real.

Believe what you want, but don't worry, she will think you are crazy before this is over.

Cindy was starting to feel a bit nervous again. Clearly, her dissociative system was not on board with this conversation, but she really needed someone to know, someone to understand, so she continued.

"Well, it's kind of hard to explain." She adjusted her position in her chair again. "You see, my shame made me feel like I deserved bad things." She paused. Angela was still listening. "Because I was bad." One more pause. Cindy expected Angela to jump in and correct her and give her scriptures to the contrary, but she didn't. She was just listening. "That changed, well, it changed me."

"I can see that." Angela tilted her head. "You do seem different today. In a good way, of course." She took another drink and smiled.

Different?

Can she see us?

What does she see?

How are we different!

This isn't good.

We can't be different, not now, not ever!

"What do you mean different?" Cindy's voice was shaking. She knew Angela meant that as a compliment, but her entire system was panicking for some reason.

"I just mean you seem more at peace today, more comfortable, I guess."

Cindy could feel herself losing control. She was slipping back into her own mind, reaching, grasping for anything to keep her present, but she couldn't get a hold.

"She switched," Michael informed the others. "The emotion was too much for her."

Big tears welled up in Cindy's eyes, and she pulled her feet up on her chair, wrapping her arms around her legs. "I'm so sorry. I didn't mean to."

Angela shifted in her seat and set her water down, "It's okay. I'm sorry, I didn't mean to upset you."

Both Cindy's and Angela's warrior angels were now beginning to fight demons. Shame was making a play for Cindy and had sent Confusion and Hopelessness to weaken her resolve.

"You didn't upset me. I was wrong." Cindy was looking down, holding her legs even tighter. "I'm sorry, I shouldn't have reacted. I know you didn't mean anything bad." Cindy's voice sounded like a little girl, and she knew it, but she couldn't change it.

Michael was sword to sword with a large demon. The being was hissing and drooling, forcing his way to Cindy. Michael met his sword blow for blow, but this entity was certainly strong. Shame was not something to be taken lightly, and he was clearly not happy that his rights for Cindy had been revoked yesterday in session.

Zral and Abei began to praise the Lord for the goodness and mercy He had shown Cindy. Their praises reached the heavens, and Angela's worshipping angels soon joined the song.

As the praise began to rise, the Holy Spirit prompted Angela to pray for Cindy. "Father God, I don't know what is happening in Cindy's heart right now, but You do. Please send Your angels to guard her and fight for her. She is Your daughter, and I know You love her deeply. You will see her through. In Jesus' name, amen."

With one more blow of Michael's sword, Shame fell to the ground.

The other demons began to scramble as the warriors' swords began to glow, and the power of the Most High God began to fill the coffee shop.

Ministering angels put a protective barrier of wings around Angela and Cindy, protecting them from the battle scene.

Angela reached across the table and squeezed Cindy's hand. "I'm here. Let's do this together."

Cindy sniffed her nose and wiped her eyes with her hand balled into a little fist. "Thank you."

Just like that, Cindy shifted again. Her feet dropped to the floor like weights, and she sat up straight as if nothing had happened. She pulled her hand back from Angela and adjusted her hair.

That was so embarrassing!

Did I really just switch her front of her?

How could that happen?

I told you she would find out you were crazy. You should have listened to me.

This isn't what was supposed to happen.

Cindy glanced around the coffee shop, looking for a reason to leave.

Just get out of here! You don't even want to know what she is thinking right now!

Leave.

Leave.

Leave!

"I have to go!" she blurted as she stood up, grabbing her purse and keys.

"So soon?" Angela stood with her.

"Yes, um... I'm sorry. I have to go." She couldn't think of a good reason why she was leaving, so she just walked out.

You are so dumb!

I can't believe you just walked out like that! If she didn't think you were crazy before, she certainly will now!

Shame was watching nearby. He wasn't allowed to be any closer because of the prayers, but he was clearly waiting for another opportunity to be let back in. Rabok and Salih kept a tight circle around Cindy while Kaleb, Hezek, and the others fought every demon trying to gain access to her heart and mind.

Stop it!

"Stop it!" Cindy almost yelled the words as she got into her car and slammed the door. "Jesus," she murmured as she collapsed on the steering wheel, tears streaming down her face.

At the name of Jesus, Michael gave Shame one final blow that sent him reeling back to where he came from. With the spirit of shame gone, the other demons were quick to retreat.

"That wasn't supposed to happen. Why did it happen?" Cindy groaned.

She cried harder than she had cried in a long time.

The tears fell for five whole minutes. Rabok and Salih stayed close by, and the warriors were all on alert in case a second attack happened. The area was quiet except for the sound of Zral and Abei lifting praises to the Lord and the painful crying pouring from Cindy's heart.

"The Holy Spirit is doing a deep work in her soul," Salih reported. "She will need rest after this."

Rabok nodded in agreement. He was ready.

Cindy's tears were subsiding.

"She is okay now." Michael sensed the Holy Spirit's presence lifting a bit. "I think the battle is over."

Cindy leaned back in the drivers' seat, her eyes clearing, and looked around the parking lot. It was as if a heavyweight was slowly lifting off her shoulders. She couldn't believe she had messed things up with Angela so badly, but she was surprised she didn't feel worse about it. Before she realized it, her phone was in her hand, and she was sending Mary a text:

> I just met with Angela. I switched right in front of her! I felt so much shame! I ran out and cried forever in my car. Now I feel at peace. I don't understand what is happening. I thought you should know.

She pressed "send" and leaned back in her seat again.

Minutes passed.

The gentle melody coming from her phone startled her out of her thoughts. It was Angela.

Don't answer it.

She didn't.

Once the call had gone to voicemail, Cindy listened to see what Angela said.

"Hi Cindy, I just wanted to tell you thanks for meeting with me today. I always enjoy chatting with you. I will be praying the Lord helps you with those boundaries with your parents. Let's try to get together again next week. Okay? See you at church this weekend!"

Another tear ran down Cindy's face, but she wasn't sure why.

Salih smiled at the release of emotion she was experiencing. The Lord was bringing healing through those tears.

She started the car and headed for home.

I need a nap.

A nap can't fix what's wrong with you.

Maybe not, but I am going to take one anyway.

The rest of the drive was quiet. Cindy was too exhausted to think.

As soon as she got home, she fell into her bed, clothes and all. Salih had stepped back, and Rabok was right by her side with rest for her body and mind. The last thing Cindy saw before her eyes closed was her clock: 3 p.m.

"She will sleep the rest of the day and into the night," Rabok stated.

Michael nodded and turned toward the rest of the troops, "Let's be sure she gets the rest she needs."

"The turmoil in her soul is great," Salih observed.

"Yes, it is, but God is healing her through the turmoil."

"The Holy Spirit was strong today with her and Angela," another commented.

"Indeed He was! It was a great show of the Lord's love for her, for them both, really. I am beginning to think that Angela is going to play a big part in Cindy's healing." Michael spoke with the confidence of someone who had seen God work in this way before.

Chapter 8

Cindy's alarm went off Wednesday at 8 a.m. She woke with a sluggish demeanor. She walked, still half asleep, into the kitchen and over to the coffee pot. She closed her eyes and took a deep breath as the smell of the coffee helped her switch more solidly into her adult self. After pouring a cup and sitting at her favorite spot overlooking the backyard, her thoughts began to awaken and join her at the table.

Yesterday was a disaster.

"Why does the day have to start with complaining," she muttered just under her breath.

You have to agree. A disaster!

It wasn't all bad.

Name something that was good!

Cindy forced herself to focus on the backyard. She didn't want to hear the complaints and ugly talk inside. She wanted to enjoy her coffee and the morning. A bluebird was sitting on the back fence again. Cindy smiled.

Bluebirds always made her happy. She wasn't sure why. Today, she felt something different when she looked at the bird. Actually, it wasn't different so much as it was identifiable. She felt love. She felt God's love for her just like she had felt it in session on Monday. She closed her eyes and breathed in deep again. It felt good.

Cindy began to think about Monday's session. It was so amazing to have the shame gone! She didn't realize how much the shame had made her take the blame for the trauma. No wonder she had been fighting the trauma all her life. She believed if she could make the trauma stop, then maybe the shame would stop too.

She paused to think about that for a moment.

"The trauma is over."

She heard it as clear as day.

"The trauma is over."

She heard it again. She felt goosebumps cover her arms and warmth in her heart. It was the Lord's voice. She knew it. She recognized it.

You can't recognize it. You are too bad to know it.

Stop!

She listened again. It was quiet in her mind. Salih had come close to her, and the Holy Spirit was working again in those deep places in her heart.

She had always viewed her trauma as what held her back. Her invisible enemy she fought every single minute of every day.

"The trauma is over." As the truth of what the Lord spoke began to sink into her heart, she realized for the first time that the trauma was truly over. The trauma was once her enemy, but it no longer existed. It was no longer happening.

She took a sip of her coffee.

The bluebird hopped from the fence to a branch on a small tree she had planted last spring. The tree had a few leaves but was mostly bare. She noticed the freedom the bluebird had. It could fly anywhere, land wherever it wanted. It didn't need to ask permission or be afraid. If someplace wasn't safe, it would just fly to a different place.

She had never been able to do that before because of the trauma.

"The trauma is over." The words rang in her spirit. The trauma was no longer happening. The only thing that existed was today. Relief washed over her as she realized she could make choices today that she could never have made in the past.

Today. This word held meaning for the first time in her life.

Today...

The bluebird flew away.

But if the trauma was not her enemy, then what was? Where should she direct her fight? There had to be a fight. She dropped her feet to the floor and set her cup on the table. Without a fight, how would she find the strength or motivation to move forward?

A picture of her parent's home flashed in her mind.

She froze in her chair for just a moment. She wasn't sure what this image meant, but the feeling it raised in her was very foreign.

Switch!

Salih stepped back and allowed her to go into autopilot mode.

Cindy stood and casually walked over to the stove to make breakfast.

"The Holy Spirit is revealing the next step of this journey to her. She will need to receive it in small pieces." Michael knew Cindy's capacity well, but he knew the Holy Spirit better. "The Lord will not overwhelm her with this."

"What did the Lord show her?" Kaleb questioned.

"I don't know, but we will find out soon enough."

"What if she forgets?"

"She has already forgotten," Michael observed as he watched Cindy fry an egg. "But the Lord will bring it back."

Cindy finished her breakfast and headed to her room to shower and dress for her job interview. It had been quite a few months since she had last worked. She was grateful to her landlord for giving her a break on rent when she quit her job a few months ago. The stress and shame of her past trauma had made getting to work almost impossible. But time and money were running out, and she needed to find a new job soon.

The blow dryer helped to drown out her thoughts as she ran a comb through her freshly washed hair.

In less than an hour, she was on the road and headed to the local department store for her interview.

This job is so demeaning!

You didn't get a graduate degree to work in a clothing store!

We have to do this. We need money!

Money? Whatever. Just be pathetic. It seems to have worked for you this far.

Shut up!

She is doing the best she can.

The chatter went on and on for the length of the drive. Cindy listened to some, but she mostly blocked out her other parts and their opinions as she drove. She needed this job, and she needed to present well at the interview to get it.

"Hello, I'm here to see Mrs. Watson." Cindy tugged on her suit jacket as the receptionist took down her name and motioned for her to sit in the waiting area.

The wait was beginning to become unbearable when Mrs. Watson finally came out from a side door. She was about the same age as Cindy, maybe a little younger. She was dressed in a professional-looking maxi dress with a wide belt, sophisticated heels, and a long silver chain around her neck. Cindy did a double-take as she noticed under Mrs. Watson's brown hair were a set of bluebird earrings! She sat stunned for a moment.

"Hello, Cindy?"

"Um... oh, hello. Mrs. Watson?" Cindy fumbled with her purse and notebook as she stood to greet her interviewer. "I love your earrings." She didn't mean to say it, but she couldn't help it.

"Oh." Mrs. Watson's hand automatically touched her ear. "Thank you." She turned toward the offices. "This way, please."

They both began to walk down the hall.

Don't blow it!

Then don't talk!

Cindy waved her hand in the air as if swatting a pesky fly. She couldn't afford to allow her parts to ruin this for her.

"Did you do a perimeter check?" Michael questioned Kaleb.

"Yes, sir. All clear. In fact, it's really clear. I think the Lord is dwelling here. There is a large angelic troop stationed throughout the building."

"Interesting," Michael nodded. "I'm curious to see what the Lord has in mind."

The angelic troops were strategically stationed around the building and with Cindy to keep things calm, just in case.

Michael followed Cindy into the office and watched as she settled into an oversized green chair adjacent to Mrs. Watson's desk. The office was bright and pleasant. Cindy could see trees just outside the window, lining the parking lot where she had parked her little blue Toyota. The sun was shining into the room, reflecting off the various knick-knacks and décor. The office was neat and tidy, without any clutter or dust. Cindy thought Mrs. Watson must be pretty stiff, given her professional appearance and her perfectly arranged office, but the atmosphere in the room was comfortable and relaxed.

"So, you are here for the sales representative job?" Mrs. Watson was looking at some papers in a file as she asked the question.

"Um... yes. I mean, that is what I was thinking."

Keep it together, guys! We have to get through this interview!

Where is my professional part! I need to be a professional right now!

Cindy's demeanor shifted.

"Yes, I applied for the job I saw online. I've never worked retail before, but I have a lot of experience working with people, and I believe I could do the job." She smiled confidently.

"That was a timely switch," one of the angels commented.

Mrs. Watson tilted her head and studied the file a moment. Then she set it on her desk and focused on Cindy. It wasn't an uncomfortable focus, more of a curious kind of focus.

"So, tell me about your last job. Why did you leave?"

Really? We are going to start with that?

Lie! Just lie! You can't tell her the truth. You just can't!

Don't lie. Don't lie! We don't want to be bad!

You need this job.

Keep it together!

"Well, it's a little complicated," Cindy whispered a prayer under her breath.

In an instant, Salih was by her side, allowing her heart to be at peace. She had no awareness of him, but his work was evident by her calmness and honesty.

"I really enjoyed my job, but I was going through some personal things, and I just needed to take a break for a while."

"You seem a bit overqualified for a retail position." Mrs. Watson's eyes were soft but direct.

"I suppose I might be, but I want to start back into the work world slowly. You know, make sure I am okay to keep up with it now."

"I see." She opened the file again.

You blew it! You just blew it!

Mrs. Watson's eyes met Cindy's again. Cindy unconsciously smoothed out a few wrinkles in her skirt and fiddled with her necklace.

"I can appreciate someone who knows their limits and sets healthy boundaries. I called your previous employers, and they had nothing but good to say about you. While I still think you are a bit overqualified for this position, I can understand where you are coming from. I'd love to give you an opportunity to get back into the work world. When can you start?"

Cindy was momentarily stunned. She didn't expect it to be this easy. "Um... Monday. I could start Monday."

"Fine. That will be fine."

"Oh, one thing."

Mrs. Watson paused.

"I need Thursday afternoons off for..."

Don't say therapy. Don't say therapy!

"I have an ongoing appointment on Thursdays, and I need those afternoons off. Will that be okay?" Cindy cringed, waiting for the response.

"That should be fine." Mrs. Watson picked up the phone and spoke with the receptionist briefly.

"Carol will show you out." Carol popped into the office as if responding to a perfectly timed cue. "Be here Monday morning at eight, and we will start your training."

"Thank you. I really appreciate this opportunity." Cindy stood, adjusted her suit jacket again, and followed Carol out the door and back to the front lobby. After a brief exchange, Cindy headed to her car.

Her head was spinning. She couldn't believe what had just happened! A job! Did she really just get a job? She didn't remember it ever being so easy. As she sat in her car, she found herself texting Mary:

I got the job! Can you believe it? I got the job!

It will never last!
You don't know that.
I know your past, and so I know your future. Nothing changes. It will never last.

Cindy swatted at the voices again. She could feel a mix of excitement and worry flowing through her. It was starting to overtake her mind and heart. She decided to stop at the coffee shop to treat herself to her favorite caramel frappuccino as a celebration and to get her mind off of, well, off of her mind!

Her usual parking spot was available. As she shifted her car into park and climbed out, she could feel the warmth of the sun on her face and shoulders. It felt so good. She stopped for a moment to take it in. Then she headed for the front door. Her angelic band was in tow behind. Michael had already sent Kaleb and Hezek to check ahead. They had come back with an "all clear" report.

The coffee shop felt different today. Cindy looked around the room as she waited in line to place her order. Somehow it felt brighter. She could hear pleasant voices around her—various conversations happening at this table and that. She had never noticed this before.

It was her turn to order. "I'll have a caramel frappuccino and a double-chocolate cookie," she said with a smile.

Who ordered the cookie?

It wasn't Cindy. It must've been a little one.

She paid the cashier and moved toward a tall table to wait for her order. As she waited, she looked around the room to put faces to the conversations she was hearing.

This is what it must be like to be present, she thought to herself. *I like it.* She smiled. It was nice to hear her own thoughts for once instead of listening to her parts and their conversations. A chuckle slipped through her lips. She could almost hear Mary saying, "Your parts *are* you; their thoughts *are* your own." She smiled. Of course, they were, and they weren't, all at the same time.

"Cindy! Your order is ready." The barista placed her cup and pastry on the counter. She frowned. She asked for it "to-go," but instead, it was neatly placed on a plate with a napkin tucked under the edge.

"Oh, well," she thought, "it is relaxing here. I could stay for a few minutes."

She found a corner booth where she could keep her back to the wall and scan the room while she munched on her cookie.

In the corner booth across the room, a little girl and her mom appeared to be having a coffee date. The little girl was dressed a bit like a teen with her jeans, stylish boots, and trendy top. Cindy could see her imitating her mom's movements, trying to look grown-up.

Cindy cringed. That scene was painful, although Cindy wasn't sure why.

Over by the fireplace, five middle-aged ladies were drinking coffee and eating pastries together. They each had a book and notepad in front of them. Maybe it was a book club or a Bible study. Two of the ladies seemed to dominate the conversation while the rest listened, contributing their thoughts here and there. She couldn't hear everything they were saying, but something about "drama" and "relationships." Cindy smiled at how those two words often came together.

I feel so different today. I wonder why.

Nothing has changed.

She waved her hand in the air.

Her cookie was almost gone. She pulled out her napkin to wipe her hands. As she glanced back up, she saw Angela. Angela was there at the coffee shop. Cindy froze. Unable to move or speak, she just stared at the door.

What is she doing here?

What do you mean? It's a coffee shop. We know she comes here. We met her here.

I know, but why is she here now?

I can't see her! Not now. Not like this?

Like what? Weren't you just saying you felt so very different today?

Shut up!

A quick scan of the room revealed there was no place to hide. While this booth allowed her to see everyone in the room, it also made her an easy target for everyone else to see.

We will have to remember this next time when we pick our spot!

I have to get out of here!

Just play it cool. Maybe she won't...

"Cindy? Cindy, is that you?"

Too late.

Angela was making her way over to the table.

Get it together, Cindy!

Cindy finished wiping off her hands and stood to greet Angela.

"Hi, Angela. Funny seeing you here." She mustered an awkward smile.

Angela gave her a quick hug. "I'm just running in for a quick minute. My husband is in the car, and we are on our way to a board meeting."

Thank goodness!

"Oh, I see. Well, I don't want to keep you." Cindy started to walk away.

"Nonsense." Angela gently took her elbow. "Come wait in line with me, and we can catch up a bit while I wait for my order."

Cindy reluctantly agreed.

"I had a job interview today." The words seemed to blurt out of Cindy's mouth.

"Really? Great! How did it go?"

"It went well. I mean, I thought it went well. I got the job."

"Congratulations! That is great news!"

Angela hugged her again, and Cindy heard someone give an irritated groan inside.

"I didn't realize you were looking for a job."

The conversation paused while Angela ordered her coffee, and the two made their way back to the corner booth where Cindy had left her coffee and what was left of her double-chocolate cookie. Somehow it didn't seem quite as appealing as it did before.

"Where will you be working?"

"Oh, it's just a department store job. You know, selling clothes and things."

"Sounds fun! I bet you'll meet a lot of interesting people in that job."

Cindy hadn't thought about the customers coming in, only the work she would be doing. She started to feel some anxiety rising in her stomach, and she did her best to push it back down.

"Probably," was all she could say.

"Angela! Your order is ready."

Saved by the barista.

I'll have to tip him before I leave.

"Oh, that's me!" Angela stood, and Cindy stood with her. "We still need to schedule that coffee again soon." She smiled and hugged Cindy one more time.

"Okay." Cindy gave her a loose hug back. "Good luck with the board meeting," was all she could think to say.

Angela grabbed her order and headed to the door, turning one last time to motion a goodbye nod before heading out to her car.

Cindy sunk into the booth.

That was so stupid! "Good luck with the board meeting!" Who says that?

Why did she have to be here?

I liked the hug.

Stupid!

Cindy was done. The day had started well. She was happy about getting a job, but now she was feeling very anxious over the thought of having to interact with strangers all day long. What if they were rude or mean? She wouldn't be able to get away from them! What if her mom came? What if her dad came? She would have to help them. There would be nowhere to hide.

Cindy started to feel her insides crumble, and she knew she had to get to the car and fast! She left her coffee and cookie crumbs behind as she darted out of the building and into the safety of her little blue Toyota.

In her car, she cried. Cindy cried hard, but she didn't really know why.

Rabok and Salih were both right by her side. They gave her the space and safety to let the tears flow. Although the Holy Spirit was present, Cindy could not sense Him. All of the heavenly beings knew more tears needed to come. Tears that had been bottled up for far too long.

Michael sent Kaleb and Hezek to stand guard around the car in case any evil would try to take advantage of this moment. Then he instructed three others to canvas the parking lot to deter any distractions that might hinder her from letting go of all that needed to be released.

The Holy Spirit continued to work in her heart, and she cried all the more.

There were no words for the pain. No memories or thoughts to attach to it. Not even a defined feeling. Just tears and pain.

Salih continued to create space for the Holy Spirit to do His work in her heart.

After several minutes, the hard sobbing began to wane and make way for the quiet tears to flow. It was as if her body was too exhausted to continue to push the deep pain to the surface, but what was already loose still needed to be released. Rabok was allowing for rest.

The ministering angel's job was a beautiful cycle of emotion and rest that cooperated with the Holy Spirit's movements.

The Holy Spirit stayed with her comforting her and encouraging the continued release of the pain and emotion that had been hidden away in her physical body for so many years.

"Her pain is deep," Salih observed.

"It is," Rabok agreed, "but she is finding the strength to release it."

"The Holy Spirit is supernaturally giving her access to this pain," Michael explained to some of the troops nearby. "The pain is too blocked for her to get there on her own." He smiled. "God knew how to orchestrate this moment gently. Releasing this pain is a gift to her. It will make her healthier and allow her to continue to grow in strength."

"So, this whole day was orchestrated?" an angel asked.

"The Lord knew what would happen, and He chose to use it to further her healing." Michael looked towards Cindy. "She felt safe and secure from the interview, enough so that she could feel calm and at peace. This is rare for her. The coffee shop is a safe place for her, so she was able to let some of her walls down in there."

The other angels nodded in agreement. "We did notice that. What else?" they asked, curious about what

Michael's experience serving the Lord had allowed him to see that they had missed.

"Seeing the little girl with her mother brought up the grief of a lost childhood. Then the book club talking about drama and relationships reminded her of the work she has had to put into any relationship she has ever had."

"And then came Angela," Hezek commented from outside of the car.

"Exactly. Then came Angela." Michael was still smiling. "The perfectly timed stop for coffee allowed Cindy to experience the new healthy relationship that the Lord is bringing her into. She is cared for by Angela in a way she has never experienced before. In many ways, it is painful to her, but that is because it is new."

"And here we are." The angels directed their attention back to Cindy. They could feel the intensity of the Holy Spirit lifting, and what was left of Cindy's tears were drying on her face.

The box of tissues Cindy kept on the backseat floor was almost empty. She fished out the last few and blew her nose. She wiped her eyes with her suit sleeve without giving any thought to her makeup or her professional attire. Tired and thoughtless, she started the car and headed home.

When she got there, she curled up on the couch and fell fast asleep.

There was no need for Michael to assign stations to his troops. This particular group of angels had been together caring for Cindy for more than a decade now. It was fascinating to finally begin to understand her as the Lord worked to bring her healing. Each of them fell into their normal positions, standing guard, providing support, and worshiping the Most High God.

When the home was quiet in times like these, and Cindy was resting, the angels all joined Zral and Abei, singing praises to the Lord of His greatness and mercy. Abei led out in song:

> Come, let's sing for joy to the Lord,
> Let's shout joyfully to the rock of our salvation.
> Let's come before His presence with a song of thanksgiving,
> Let's shout joyfully to Him in songs with instruments.

"Psalm 95[1]," Michael nodded. "This is a good one."
The other angels began to join in.

> For the Lord is a great God
> And a great King above all gods,
> In whose hand are the depths of the earth,
> The peaks of the mountains are also His.
> The sea is His, for it was He who made it,

And His hands formed the dry land.
Come, let's worship and bow down,
Let's kneel before the Lord, our Maker.

The melody was slow and steady with a rhythm that carried their voices to the very throne room of God. As their voices reached the presence of the Ancient of Days, the worshipping angels around the throne began to join in the Psalm.

The light of the Holy One began to fill Cindy's humble home. The presence of the Lord was thick and drove the angels to bow in worship.

Come, let's sing for joy to the Lord,
Let's shout joyfully to the rock of our salvation.
Let's come before His presence with a song of thanksgiving,
Let's shout joyfully to Him in songs with instruments.
For the Lord is a great God
And a great King above all gods,
In whose hand are the depths of the earth,
The peaks of the mountains are also His.
The sea is His, for it was He who made it,
And His hands formed the dry land.
Come, let's worship and bow down,
Let's kneel before the Lord, our Maker.

The presence of the Lord that had settled in the home was so strong that evil would not dare to come near. Such a strong presence did not happen often, and it would not last long. Michael and his troops rested in the sovereignty of their Commander-in-Chief.

Michael had the sense that the Lord was very pleased with the freedom Cindy was receiving. After a few moments, the heat of His presence began to return to heaven. The room returned to its normal state. The angelic army stood and saluted their General, Jesus Christ. All felt deep regard for their position in this army as they moved back into their positions around Cindy's home.

Cindy's sleep was sweet that night. She slept deep, and she would certainly wake up feeling refreshed and ready for her day.

Chapter 9

She had her regular Thursday appointment with Mary, and she was anxious to tell her about her new job and the run-in with Angela. It seemed like there was something else that had happened since the session on Monday, but she had no idea what it was.

The drive to Mary's office was uneventful. The weather was turning cooler with fall approaching, and Cindy enjoyed it. Generally, the summer's heat was hard on her until the middle to late fall, but September was usually a good month. She smiled at the many trips and adventures she had experienced in September throughout the years.

One time, four or five years ago, she drove to the Grand Canyon just because she could. She had never seen it before, and she had some time off work. It was such a relaxing and peaceful drive—just her and the Lord. That was a year before her healing journey took off. The months following her trip were intense and frightening. She was yet to have any memories of the spiritual abuse she encountered as a child, and in that season, they were leaking from her memory into her reality. At least, that was how Mary had explained it.

It was a year after those memories started "leaking" before she even met Mary. She saw three other counselors before she landed in Mary's office. None of the other counselors had any idea what to do with her. They tried their best, but they just didn't understand. To that point, Cindy had graduated college, lived on her own, and been a successful businesswoman. Two counselors believed she had a mental breakdown from stress, and the third counselor implied she was just seeking attention. She was about to give up when she decided to give a counselor recommended by her church a try. Being in Mary's office for the first time and hearing her explain what Cindy was going through was like water in the desert.

"Thank You, God, for bringing me into Mary's office that day," Cindy whispered as she was recounting her journey.

Cindy could only feel a little bit of the gratitude she knew was there, but that was okay. Mary had taught her that it was very healthy for her brain to express gratitude out loud whether she had an actual feeling attached to it or not.

"So grateful," she said again.

As her car came to a stop in the small parking lot outside of Mary's office, Cindy closed her eyes to pray.

"Lord, I don't know what You have planned for me today. I don't even really understand what You have done for me up to this point, but I am grateful. I am grateful just to know You are near, and You are helping me." She paused to think about her next words. "I know this may be a lot to ask, but if You could just send an angel or two to be with me today, I could use the help. I am so very tired." Another pause. "Above all, though, I trust You with my journey. Amen."

"If she only knew," one of the angels responded.

"True," another angel commented. "It would have been impossible for her to survive this far if the Lord hadn't dispatched us to be by her side along the way."

"Praise be to the Most High God!" they all said in unison, and they felt His pleasure with His daughter.

Cindy settled into the waiting room of Mary's office. It was comfortable here. Not just physically but emotionally. She knew the work would be hard, and she didn't like that, but she knew her heart would be cared for.

Mary appeared in the hallway. "I'm ready for you, Cindy." She smiled the welcoming smile that Cindy was accustomed to. It was nice to be here.

As she sat on the familiar green couch in Mary's office, her angelic band took their places in and around the office. Michael and Ronan greeted one another, and Ronan adjusted his troops to account for Michael's group. While Michael and Ronan had the same rank, Ronan called the shots in Mary's office since this was his jurisdiction assigned by the Most High God.

Gabe was nearby and gave Michael and his group a warm, welcoming nod.

Mary opened the session in prayer and then settled into her high-back chair with her notepad on her lap and a pen in her hand. "So, tell me about your week," she began.

"I don't remember much about the week, but I do remember yesterday."

"Okay, let's start there."

Cindy took her through the day from the job interview, the strange feelings in the coffee shop, the run-in with Angela, and the intense sobbing in her car. She talked about her deep sleep last night and the drive to Mary's office.

"It sounds like the Lord has been working this week," Mary confirmed.

"I suppose so," Cindy hesitated, "I just don't understand what is happening. I don't know what is going on."

"How have your parts been?" Mary inquired. "They are usually pretty expressive on your way into session."

It was then Cindy realized she hadn't heard much from her parts since her nap yesterday. "I'm not sure." She listened to her mind. "They have been quiet since yesterday."

"Interesting." Mary jotted it down. "Why don't we pray and ask the Lord about it."

"Okay."

Both Mary and Cindy closed their eyes. The room was quiet for a few moments before Mary began to pray. "Dear Lord, thank You for the tremendous battles You are fighting on behalf of Cindy. Your power and sovereignty have allowed her to become free from things she never thought possible. We are so grateful for Your love and mercy toward her."

Mary paused as a shift in the atmosphere of the room became apparent.

Ronan noticed a dark cloud settling outside the office window, not one that could be seen in the natural, but a spiritual darkness. He motioned one of his warriors to move closer to the window to keep watch. Michael did the same, and Hezek was by the window in an instant.

"As we come into Your presence, God, we surrender to You our motives and agenda for being here. We want to be aligned with You and with Your purpose for this time. Please show us where You would like to begin."

Mary and Cindy were quiet for a few moments, waiting on the Lord.

A bolt of lightning, then the crack of thunder emanated from the dark cloud, and Ronan could see a tornado forming.

"What is that?" Gabe asked.

"It has been a long time since we have seen one of these." Michael studied it for a moment. "I'm not sure about this specific tornado, but it can mean a spirit of chaos or destruction that Satan has been using to send torment and dysfunction."

Gabe looked back out the window.

"The Lord will tell us what we need to know about this one." Ronan was confident. "The good news is that if the Lord is revealing it, He will deal with it." He signaled for the troops to maintain their positions.

The warrior angels had their hands on their swords.

Salih and the other ministering angels came in close to Cindy to give her the space to connect with the Holy Spirit without interference.

Zral and Abei, along with the other worshipping angels, looked toward heaven and began to utter words of worship and praise to the Most High God.

Ronan surveyed the group and knew they would be ready for whatever the Lord had planned.

Cindy and Mary were sitting quietly, waiting on the Lord, waiting for His direction. In a slow movement extending from the storm outside the building, through the walls, and into the room, a shake began to take over the space.

Cindy could not feel it. She had a holy buffer put in place by the ministering angels.

Mary felt it in her spirit. She intuitively moved her hand to the armrest as if to steady herself even though the physical room had not moved at all.

"Cindy, the Lord wants to deal with something strong today. A force that has been tormenting you for a long time."

Cindy nodded in agreement, with her head still bowed and her eyes squeezed shut.

"Tell me what the Lord is showing you," Mary requested.

Cindy was quiet, and Mary waited patiently.

"I see a storm. The clouds are dark. I think there is rain; I'm not sure." Cindy cringed. "There is a tornado. I thought it was just forming, but now that I look, I think it has been there all along, and I just couldn't see it."

She was silent a few more minutes, and then Mary heard her let out a long breath.

"I know this is intense, Cindy. You are doing a great job. Stay with me now." She waited a moment to make sure Cindy was okay and still mentally present. Cindy gave a quick nod. Her body was tense, but she was staying present.

"Father God, what do You want Cindy to know about this storm?"

The angelic guard was motionless, waiting for the signal that the fight was beginning. So far, there was no demonic movement from the storm, nothing to battle, just the sense of the evil seeping out of the cloud and building in the tornado.

Cindy was motionless as well. After a moment, she tilted her head as if she was listening to something. "I see the tornado is connected to something in the dark cloud. I can't quite tell what it is." She paused again, listening intently. "I feel God showing me that this tornado has been the cause of the confusion in my life. My failures, my inability to make decisions, the confusion I have had in relationships, all of it. It was all created by this tornado. He wants to disconnect this from me, but He says it won't be easy."

Cindy was quiet for a few moments again. Her eyes were still closed as she waited to see what else the Lord would show her.

Suddenly, her chest began to heave as her breathing got heavy.

"Can you tell me what is happening?" Mary asked gently.

"There are pictures, images circling through my mind. They are terrible, terrible." She winced, and her body tensed as if she experienced a blow.

"Father God, please put a guard around this office and prohibit Satan from speaking or interfering with what You are doing."

At that, Ronan and the angelic troops saw their swords began to glow. The faith-filled prayer from Mary's spirit had fueled them and revealed the evil spirit whispering and harassing Cindy. The guard quickly defeated the enemies that had gained access to the room.

"The images have stopped," Cindy reported as her body relaxed.

Ronan reshuffled the army to keep the rest of the enemy outside of the room.

Other angels began to come from all directions to join in the battle.

"Cindy?" Mary waited. "Are you still with me?"

"I am."

"We need to ask the Lord again about the tornado." Another pause. "Are you able to do that with me?"

Cindy nodded without opening her eyes.

"Father God, what do You want Cindy to know about this tornado?"

The dark cloud had settled around the office. The angels could no longer see outside the office window. Warrior angels now battled in the darkness outside the walls of the office. The sound of metal clashing and evil fighting was getting loud. "We must stand firm in the confidence of the Most High God," Michael proclaimed. "He is allowing this battle to come to us so Satan may be defeated!"

"Praise the Most High!" the angel band said in unison.

"I think I see something," Cindy started. "I see... Jesus. It looks like Jesus."

"Where is He?"

"He is above the storm." Cindy was determined to find her way through this. "I think He wants me to join Him."

"Are you willing?" Mary was taking notes as Cindy was talking.

"Yes, but I don't know. Oh! I am with Him now. He brought me up." Cindy was still again. The quietness of the room that Mary and Cindy were experiencing was quite contrary to the spiritual battle happening all around them.

"Tell me what you hear or see, Cindy."

Darkness was continuing to seep through the walls into the room. The worshipping angels moved closer to the walls and lifted their faces to the heavens as they sang worship to the God on High. The dark steam around them started to evaporate.

"Jesus says I must do something very hard," Cindy began. "He promises He will help me, but I have to do it. He cannot do it for me."

Michael could feel faith coming from Cindy's heart as she listened to her Savior.

"I see a little girl. She looks just like I did when I was five years old. She looks sad and tired." Cindy took a deep, slow breath. "She just climbed up on Jesus's lap, and she is resting against His chest." Just for an instant, a small smile formed on Cindy's face. Then she continued, "The tornado was made by a generational line. I can see the tornado when it first started ten generations ago. It was small but black and dangerous. Over the decades, it has grown in size and strength. Today, it could wipe out entire cities in a blink of an eye."

Cindy was quiet again. Jesus was just watching the storm with her, taking it all in.

"How is His demeanor?" Mary inquired.

"He is calm, peaceful. It is as if the storm isn't even dangerous to Him." Cindy felt disconnected from what was happened. She was simply reporting the information as she saw it in her mind's eye.

"Does the storm seem dangerous to you, Cindy?" Mary asked at the prompting of the Holy Spirit.

Cindy observed it for a moment. "Yes. It looks deadly."

Mary simply nodded.

Cindy stared at it for a moment. "I can't believe I have survived it."

"You survived it because of the power of God in you," Mary replied.

Cindy looked back at the storm. "I don't feel like I am surviving it. I feel like it is killing me."

Her attention was drawn back to Jesus and the little version of herself sitting with Him. She could tell He was listening to every word her heart was saying. The little one adjusted in His lap. He wrapped an arm around her, and she nestled her head on His shoulder.

Mary continued, "This storm has been draining life away from you. It wanted more life, but the heavenly Father would not allow it. Now that the spirits of death and shame are gone, I believe the Lord wants to severe this storm from you and your bloodline."

"I want that!" the words flew from her mouth. "Jesus, how do we severe this?"

A picture of her parent's house flashed in her mind again, and then the whole scene was gone.

Cindy slowly opened her eyes.

Mary waited while Cindy's eyes adjusted to the room.

The darkness outside was now being restrained by an invisible force.

"Are you okay?" Mary asked.

"I am," Cindy responded. "That was a lot."

Mary wrote a few more notes on her notepad while waiting on Cindy.

"I saw a picture of my parent's house at the end; you know, before everything went black. It reminded me that I saw that same picture a few days ago when I was praying."

"What does that mean to you?" Mary inquired.

"Well, I think the Lord is telling me that this tornado is coming from my parents, my bloodline, and He wants to sever it."

"I think you may be right."

Cindy thought about it for a moment, "I think I need to stop seeing them. Not just stop seeing them, but stop talking to them, stop everything." Her hands were trembling. She heard the words coming from her mouth, but she couldn't believe them. She didn't want them, and yet, at the same time, she desperately needed them.

"What do you think it would be like to set these kinds of boundaries with your parents?"

"I'm not sure." Cindy thought about it. "I know right now I have so much anxiety every time I even think about them. If I have to talk to them on the phone or even see a text come through from them, I can have an instant panic attack."

"It must be difficult to have parents like that," Mary affirmed.

"It is, well it would be, I mean," Cindy stammered, trying to find the words. "What I mean is, they may have given birth to me, but they are not really parents. Not parents like God wanted parents to be. They are just the man and woman who raised me."

Mary listened as Cindy put her feelings into words.

"I have so many painful memories with them. The abuse, the trauma were terrible, but even in the day-to-day, I was miserable. Every day I was living a lie. Pretending to be a happy, Christian family, and then the doors would close, and the darkness would choke me—" She turned to stare out the window. "Every day."

A single tear ran down Cindy's face. She quickly wiped it away and looked back in Mary's direction. "I don't think I have ever cried about this before." She thought again. "I have had full-on panic attacks, deep bouts of depression, and anger outbursts, but I don't think I have ever actually cried." A few more tears ran down her face, and she let them fall.

"It seems like you have reached a new place in this journey." Mary gave her a warm smile to validate her thoughts and feelings.

"I think I have. I realized for the first time that my parents and all of this generational evil are the real enemies here. My parts, my dissociation, it saved me from them—as much as possible anyways—it's not bad, *they* are bad."

Mary waited a moment. "So, what do you want to do about this?"

"I know I need to sever the relationship, but I am going to have to think about it for a while," Cindy said numbly.

"I know," Mary replied. "This is a big decision."

"Will Jesus wait for me?"

"Of course, He will! He understands what this will mean, and He knows how hard it will be." Mary smiled. "He will be ready when you are."

Cindy nodded. "I am so tired. Is it time to go yet?"

Mary glanced at the clock. "It is. Let's wrap up in prayer."

As Mary and Cindy bowed their heads to pray, Ronan, Michael, and the angelic troops praised the Lord together. The storm was being restrained, Cindy was finding healing, and they were worshipping their Commander for all He had done.

When Mary finished praying, she and Cindy said their goodbyes, and Ronan and Michael did the same.

Cindy's drive home was quiet, other than her own thoughts. Whatever parts had been quiet since the day before now had plenty to say about the session.

There may be hope now.

I never knew how bad my parents were.

I have to end things now before it is too late!

Sever relationship with your parents! Are you crazy?

There is no way they will let you do that.

Someone inside was crying.

You would have to move to Africa for that to happen.

I need my mommy!

Shut up! Your mommy never loved you.

The crying intensified.

You baby!

The chatter went on and on for the entire drive home. Somehow the voices were clearer and more distinct today than Cindy had ever noticed before, and that crying, was it new? She didn't remember it. She did know they were loud. It was like she was sitting in a room with them.

We have already lost too much. We can't lose the parents too. Then we will all be gone.

That statement stopped her. "What?" Cindy wasn't sure what she was hearing. She didn't know what that meant. "We will all be gone?" Anxiety started to well up in her stomach. Just as soon as she noticed it, it was gone.

The rest of the drive home was quiet internally as well as externally.

As Cindy was preparing dinner later that evening, the phone rang. She let it go to voicemail. It was Angela, again.

Why doesn't she give up? Doesn't she know you're not worth it?

Shut up!

The sound of her phone ringing again jolted her out of the conversation. She grabbed the phone only to drown out the thoughts in her mind.

"Hello?"

"Hi, um... Angela?" Cindy knew she sounded timid. She didn't mean to.

"Hi, Cindy! How are you?" There it was again—that happy-to-see-me sound in her voice.

I want my mommy.

Cindy froze.

Speak! She is going to think you are so stupid!

"I'm sorry, I think I lost signal for a moment," she lied. "I saw you called?"

"Oh, yes, I did." Angela cleared her throat. "I am hosting a ladies' breakfast this weekend, and I thought you might like to join us."

"You are?"

That was a dumb thing to say.

She is doing her best. Shut up!

"Yes, I am. Just a few ladies, maybe five or six. We will eat and talk about the weather, plans everyone has this autumn, whatever comes to mind. It's very casual."

Cindy was quiet. She wasn't really sure what to say.

Angela continued, "You don't have to bring anything. You don't even have to talk. I just thought you might like to meet some other ladies from the church, and this would be a great opportunity."

Did she plan this whole thing so I could meet people?

Don't be stupid. She doesn't care that much!

Of course, she did! She is tired of you and wants to pass you off to someone else.

"Yes!" Cindy practically shouted. She didn't mean to. She just wanted the voices to stop.

"Wonderful! I will text you the details. See you then!"

The room suddenly felt very silent without Angela's cheery voice in Cindy's ear. Even her parts were quiet for a moment. And just for a very brief moment, Cindy could feel the hollowness in her own heart. As soon as she felt it, it was gone.

"God is moving through Angela," Michael told the group. "Be on alert."

The troops stood at alert, but there was an extra holy reverence in the room as they all let Michael's words sink in. "God is moving." Of course, He was always moving, but when His movements came into their awareness, something special always happened.

Chapter 10

Throughout the day on Friday, Cindy could not shake the feeling of abandonment she was experiencing. It was very different than she had ever felt before, though. For most of her life, she felt abandoned by her parents and others. Today, she could feel the reality of her abandoning her parents, and it felt awful.

Thoughts of her mother's sadness and her father's anger swirled through her mind. She wondered what they would think of her, and she feared them, thinking she was a terrible, ungrateful daughter.

Her mind was racing from the moment she got out of bed.

They can never understand you, and they never will, a bitter voice retorted in her mind.

Understand her? They don't need to understand her! They are the parents; she just needs to obey them.

She tried to run a few errands, but the relentless banter in her mind never stopped.

Obey them! The voices had gone from bitter to angry. *Do you even remember what they did? What they put us through?*

She squeezed her eyes shut as she pulled back into her driveway. She couldn't take much more. The guilt, the pain, the disgust she felt about herself was overwhelming.

It doesn't matter. They are the parents. They know what is best. The voices continued as she unpacked the few groceries she could buy before the madness in her mind drove her out of the store.

Best? There was nothing best about what they did. They deserve to be cut off!

A small voice was crying again.

Cindy didn't know what to do. She knew what she needed to do, but she was afraid, afraid there would be consequences and that they would be dire.

She briefly noticed she was in her pajamas, tucked in her bed with the soft green blanket from the living room clutched to her chest. For a split second, she wondered how she got there. Then the next wave of fear and guilt struck her, and she pulled the blanket over her face.

Of course, there will be consequences! They aren't just going to let her go.

If you do this, it will be the end. The voice was so convincing.

If you don't do this, you won't make it. This voice was more than convincing. This voice felt like a fact. Something she knew in the depths of her being. She had to do something.

Unbeknownst to her, Zral and Abei had been singing praises to the Most High God since her session with Mary had ended the day before. Their worship was aiding to strengthen the restraints to the storm that raged just out of reach of her.

Rabok and Salih had stayed close to her since the session. They had allowed her to hear only the voices of her own heart as she struggled with the reality of what must be done. They had given her rest from the intense emotions through sleep and a variety of perfectly timed distractions to take her away from her thoughts.

Kaleb and Hezek had kept the pestering demons at bay who had tried to speak words of discouragement and despair to her. Samson and Jason had even returned to assist in the battle after the most recent session.

Nothing had come to Cindy's mind that wasn't of the Lord or her own soul. The Most High God knew that this next decision would be huge, and she needed supernatural intervention to make it. It had to be made on her own, but He would help keep her decision free from the influence of the enemy.

Chapter 11

On Saturday morning, Cindy was getting ready for the ladies' breakfast at Angela's house when a messenger angel flew into her home with a message for Michael. After a few moments of private conversation, the messenger left, and Michael turned to address the group.

"The Sovereign Lord has seen to it that we are made aware of what is going to happen next." The troops awaited the news. "Cindy's parents have been trying to contact her for the last week. Up until now, the Lord has intervened and made them unsuccessful."

"Praises be!" shouted a few of the angels.

"Amen," Michael agreed. "The time has come for Him to allow them to make contact. Cindy is struggling with the decision to break ties with her family. She needs to experience the relationship with them with her new level of awareness so her decision will be clear."

"What is our assignment?" Hezek asked.

"The same as always. We are to protect her. The Lord is lifting His hand from separating them, but *not* from His protection of her. He will do this in a safe way."

The troops nodded. They understood.

"When will this happen?" Kaleb asked.

"I do not have that information, so we will just continue to protect Cindy in all of the ways we have been."

"Praise be to the Most High God!" the angels said in unison as Zral and Abei continued their song to the Lord.

As they sang, Cindy finished getting ready for the ladies' breakfast and headed to the driveway.

As she slipped into the front seat of her car, she realized she was holding her breath. For the first time in her life, she had come to recognize her desperate need for a strong, consistent relationship. She wanted it to be with her parents. But at the same time, she knew it never could be.

Her relationship with Angela was intriguing to her. As an adult, she admired her and wanted to be friends with her. Cindy felt like she could learn and grow from Angela, and it felt nice for her to be interested in Cindy's life. However, not all of her was an adult. Her younger self-states thought and said things about Angela that were embarrassing, even shameful. Then there were the angry and hateful parts that made it difficult to feel anything positive.

Parts of Cindy wanted Angela to be her mother. They wanted Angela to hold them and tell them nice things. They wanted her love.

Cindy cringed. She hated this. She felt deep shame, and the self-states with the anger let her know how dumb she was for even thinking it.

Above her car, the warfare had begun. Michael and his troops had been battling spirits of shame coming at the vehicle from every direction since she walked out of the house. These spirits were attached to parts of Cindy's mind that had carried shame since childhood. They lived in shame and experienced shame in every situation. They carried the shame, so Cindy didn't have to—at least the Cindy that lived everyday life.

On this day, the spirit of shame was striking strong. Parts of Cindy were hiding in their own shame for their desire for comfort and love from Angela. Cindy's head was filling with chaos.

Michael stabbed two large demons through the chest with his sword.

Cindy began to cry as she pulled out on the main road to drive across town.

Samson and Jason chased a handful of demons away from the car and swatted them as they poofed away.

You'll never be anything!

You are worthless, and you know it!

Angela pities you. Do you want that? Do you want pity?

Stupid girl, your parents are the only ones who would have you!

Cindy could no longer see the road. The tears were filling her eyes and running down her face, and her mind was so full, she couldn't focus her eyes on the road. She couldn't distinguish any words or specific thoughts; she just knew her mind felt very loud.

The car swerved as Cindy almost hit the curb. Two additional ministering angels joined Rabok and Salih, sent directly from heaven to aid in the battle. They began to stabilize her emotions and allowed her to take in a few deep breaths. As the presence of the Holy Spirit began to amplify and fill the interior of the car, the worshipping angels began to sing louder.

Around the car, the angelic troops could feel the Lord's presence as their swords gave off a gentle glow. It was enough to turn the tide of the battle.

Cindy's head began to clear. Her tears slowed, and her grip tightened on the steering wheel.

The angelic troops defeated the last of the shame spirits and settled into guard positions around the vehicle.

Cindy wiped her eyes with the back of her hand then pushed in a CD by the worship team at her church.

I know I can do this! I need to do this.

Her favorite song came on, and she focused on the words with all of her energy.

The Lord has gone before me.
He will be my victory.
For in the Lord remains all power.
Praise His sovereignty!

Before she knew it, she was pulling into Angela's driveway.

As she turned off the car, she just sat and waited. Her breathing was becoming more and more steady. She didn't know exactly what she was waiting for. She just waited.

This is so dumb. Just go home. No one wants you here.

We need a person! We need someone, someone who will...

Shut up!

These voices felt more like herself. Still brutal, but nothing like the ones earlier.

We don't need anyone.

People are scary.

The soft crying started on the inside again.

"We can do this," Cindy started. Self-talk was hard and awkward, but she needed to get her thoughts unified. "I know it is hard..."

And scary.

"Yes, it is scary too, but we can do this." Cindy searched for words. "We have each other."

No way. I'm not part of them.

Cindy sighed and pushed her thoughts aside again. She could hear her thoughts fade a bit as she stepped out of the car, but she knew they were all still there. Parts of her were still reeling over that last session and the thought of setting boundaries with her parents. Others were so afraid of what might happen. Still, others believed total isolation from all people would be the only path to safety. She was tired. Tired of battling the thoughts and tired of trying to sort them out. The drive just to get here about did her in. If she wasn't so determined to find someone who could maybe, just maybe be a lifeline for when she ended things with, well, when her other relationships changed, she would have gotten back in her car and headed straight home to sleep. But she was determined.

Cindy heard her knuckles rapping at the door.

Within a few seconds, the door opened, and Angela greeted her with the usual enthusiasm and hug.

"I'm so glad you made it!"

If she only knew how close I was to abandoning it all!

"Me too," she said with a weak smile.

Angela squeezed her arm slightly as she dropped her embrace and headed into the living room; just that one tiny squeeze was enough to bring Cindy fully into the room. There was something about it. Almost as if Angela maybe did know how hard the struggle was to get here.

Salih was there, giving Cindy the security to feel the comfort of the moment. He knew the relationship with Angela was important—all of the angels did—so he increased Cindy's capacity to feel the comfort and connection just for a moment.

Hezek had just returned from a survey of the property and was giving his report to Michael. "It is as we expected," he stated.

"Excellent," replied Michael. Earlier, they had sent ahead scouts to get an idea of what they were walking into, and it looked as if nothing had changed. Michael gave assignments to each of the angels, sending them throughout the property. He assigned a few to stay near Cindy.

The Most High God had seen it fit to increase his angelic troops by almost half with this newest development in Cindy's healing journey. Michael had more than enough to handle whatever might come.

Angela's home was simple but elegant. Just like Angela, Cindy thought. The thought made her blush, but she didn't know why.

There were four other ladies in the room, paired off in conversations. It didn't look intentional, more like they were casually mingling, and that's how they ended up. Angela showed Cindy to a small buffet near the far end of the living room next to the kitchen. There were cute little pastries, boiled eggs, and a variety of fruit and crackers.

Cindy was too anxious to eat, but she made a plate to keep her hands busy and look more normal.

Normal! Whatever that is!

Please! Not now.

"Let me introduce you to everyone." Angela guided Cindy over to the first pair of ladies. "This is Samantha and Ginger. They both go to our church, although they are usually working in the Kid's Ministry, so you may not see them much."

The two exchanged pleasantries with Cindy and then continued their conversation about their tomato and pepper plants. Angela could see that Cindy wasn't really interested, so she motioned toward the other pair of ladies and walked Cindy over to meet them.

"Jackie, Bethany, this is my friend Cindy."

"Hi, Cindy!" Bethany was all smiles. It kind of took Cindy aback for a minute.

"Uh, hi. Nice to meet you."

"You as well," Jackie chirped in. "Do you know much about dogs?"

Dogs? What a strange question.

"Well, a little." Cindy stammered a bit with her response. "I had several different dogs growing up, but I don't have one now." Cindy was intrigued by such a specific question.

"Well, Bethany and I were just discussing what kind of dog is the best breed to own. She says golden retrievers, but I say Boston terriers. What do you say?"

All three ladies looked at Cindy, waiting for a response. She could feel her heart start to pound, and her palms were feeling very sweaty.

"Well, I am partial to Irish terriers," she responded, relaxing slightly. "They are affectionate and also independent. It's a good mix."

"Hmm, interesting choice," Bethany replied. "I'd still take a golden retriever, though. They are such beautiful animals!"

Cindy expected the conversation to pull away from her now, but she was surprised when Jackie had a follow-up question. "So, what kind of dogs did you own growing up?"

Like she wants to hear about your childhood! She couldn't handle it.

Just shut up.

The soft crying started again, or maybe it never really stopped.

Cindy took a deep breath and focused hard on Bethany and Jackie. She really wanted this to work. "I had several different breeds growing up," she started.

So far, so good everyone seems interested.

"When I was very small, we had two dalmatians; a brother and sister. They were a lot of fun. The girl,

Cookie, had so much energy! She was fun to chase and play with. The boy, Dashing, was so kind. He would play with Cookie and me, but mostly he would be around when I was sad or lonely."

Don't talk about that here!

Don't tell the stories! They can't know.

You must stop!

"I mean, you know, if I fell down or something," Cindy tried to make sad and lonely sound normal and not like the abuse it was when she was growing up. It must have worked because Bethany started talked about her friend's dalmatian.

Cindy noticed Angela had walked off, although she wasn't sure when. She could see her getting some papers ready for later. Cindy tried to fade away from the two chatting about their childhood pets, but they kept drawing her back in with this question or that. It was kind of nice to be included but also very scary.

There's that word again, "scary." Why does everything have to be scary?

Everything is scary!

Cindy could hear the sound of someone crying softly inside her mind.

Toughen up. You have survived worse than a conversation in a lovely house with nice people like these.

Cindy pushed the last bit of a pastry in her mouth. She wasn't sure who she was listening to most, Bethany and Jackie, or her internal self. Most of them were complaining as usual, but there were a few pictures of playful times with Cookie and Dashing that were running through her mind. It was like someone turned on a video of her childhood and played it on a big screen.

This often happened with flashbacks—which she hated—but it rarely happened with happy memories. In fact, up until this moment, she didn't think she had any happy memories.

She was smiling at the thought of Cookie pulling little Cindy across the room on a blanket when suddenly the smile fell from her face. On the big screen, she could see her mom enter the living room and swat at the dog with a rolled-up newspaper. Her mom was screaming something about the dog making a mess in the kitchen as she chased poor Cookie into the backyard. Little Cindy, still sitting on the blanket, had big tears welling up in her eyes.

Adult Cindy, sitting in Angela's house with strangers, eating pastries, suddenly realized where she was, and she jumped, startled by how different her present reality was from the memory she was reliving just a moment ago. Unfortunately, Bethany and Jackie both noticed.

"Are you okay?" Jackie asked.

"Sure, um... I'm fine." Cindy pushed her hair back behind her ear. "Just a shiver, I suppose." Cindy didn't know what to say, but again, it seemed like enough.

"So anyway," Bethany continued, "I may be swaying to thinking of getting a dalmatian after all. What do you think, Cindy?"

Cindy had no idea what they were talking about or the context of the question. She was floundering to find words when Angela's voice saved her.

"Ladies, I'd love to take a few minutes and talk about the upcoming concert at the church."

The room quieted, and Cindy took a deep breath of relief.

"As you know, we have a big worship night coming in just over a month. We have been trying to come up with a venue for the meet and greet before the concert, and I think we have just the place! A local couple owns a really nice barn on the south side of town."

Cindy's stomach sank. "It can't be," she said under her breath.

"It has everything we need," Angela continued.

"Sir, a portal is opening on the south side of the house," one of the warriors reported as he flew into the room.

"Stand your ground!" Michael instructed his troops.

"And the views are breathtaking!" Angela was still talking about the features of this "special place."

How can this be happening! This was safe. Now, now, it just can't be happening!

Quit freaking out! We don't even know if it's them or not.

Cindy's heart was pounding so hard she thought for sure everyone would hear it.

Of course, it's them. How can it not be! She just described my parent's barn to a tee.

Cindy tried to focus on Angela's words. She needed to know if it was her barn or not. Was it the place she grew up? The place where so many bad things happened when she was little. It couldn't be, but everything she said matched up.

"The portal is open wide!" a warrior angel shouted from outside the house.

"Maintain the perimeter!" Michael called back as he dispatched a few more troops to cover the outside of the house.

Angela's band of angels, combined with those of the other ladies, had all joined in the battle. A slew of demonic entities was gushing from the portal and attempting to spread in every direction. So far, the six bands of angels had held them to the area directly between the portal and the house.

The worshipping angels had lined the inside of Angela's home and were calmly singing praises to the Most High God. Each of the ministering angels sat by their assignments. Since the demons had not entered the house, there was no need for special attention from the warrior angels, but they were nearby just in case.

Cindy was a different story, though. Her heart was racing, and she felt as if she might pass out.

"Just say the name. Where is it? Where is it?" she mumbled to herself again.

"I think I have seen that place from the highway," Bethany mentioned. "Is it the old Hickory place?"

The sound of metal hitting metal outside of the house was getting louder, and the ministering angels were issuing praise to the Lord with faith and assurance.

"No, no. It's *Sutton Farms* off of 29."

She said it.

It was the last thing Cindy heard.

Chapter 12

The sun was shining through her bedroom window. She could hear a bird or two singing outside. She sleepily rubbed her eyes and rolled over on her side. After a few blinks, her eyes were open and gazing across the room.

Suddenly, she jolted up in bed.

The party! I was at the party. What happened?

Silence.

"Come on," she said out loud in her room. "What happened?"

Still silent.

"Okay. So, you talk non-stop when I am trying to get things done, but when I need information, you have nothing to say?"

"Fine!" she shouted as she threw her legs over the edge of the bed and stomped into the bathroom. "I hope you never speak again!"

She slammed the door of the bathroom, and tears began to flow in place of the anger. Why did it always end this way? Why couldn't she just stay present for one entire event? Why did her parents have to ruin everything? Where was God in this? He was supposed to be protecting her, keeping her safe from them. How could He let this happen? How could He let a church event happen on their property? In that place?

It was all too much for her to take. She sat on the bathroom floor and cried for at least an hour. She cried until she couldn't keep her eyes open anymore. The sheer exhaustion of the intense emotions was enough to put her into a deep sleep, curled up on the navy blue rug on the bathroom floor.

"She took that harder than I would have thought," Salih commented to Michael. "Generally, her emotions need a lot of coaxing to be released."

"It was what she needed," Michael responded solemnly. "Her denial about her parents was strong, and she needed something strong to happen to break it."

"The battle was fierce to keep her in the bondage. I'm so thankful God let that happen at Angela's home. We had so many reinforcements there," Kaleb chimed in.

"Agreed," Michael nodded. "The Most High God always plans perfectly. It was hard for her, but it needed to be. It was easy for us; it needed to be. The Lord knew it would be the hardest but the best place to break through this bondage."

"His sovereignty is amazing. He gave her what she needed while keeping her safe at the same time." Salih smiled.

Zral and Abei were still worshipping. They had not stopped since the portal had opened and eventually closed at Angela's house. They witnessed the power of the Lord fighting for Cindy when she could not fight for herself. They witnessed the demons fleeing in terror as the small group of ladies sang a chorus of Amazing Grace at Jackie's request, who was very sensitive to the Spirit of the Lord. They witnessed Cindy leaving for home after the song and being guided by the angels down the road and into her driveway. They witnessed Rabok bringing her rest by the power of the Lord as she fell asleep in her bed. And they witnessed the Lord gently taking what was left of the walls of denial surrounding her parents' role in her life. They witnessed the greatness of the Most High God, and they did not stop worshipping Him for it.

"Praises be to the Most High," several angels responded in unison.

When Cindy came to, it was early afternoon. She couldn't believe she had slept on the bathroom floor all that time.

Her body felt as if she had been in a war and lost. Aches and pains ran through and through, from her body to her heart, through her brain, and back again. Even her spirit felt weak.

She sat at her favorite spot in the kitchen with her coffee cup in hand and her feet pulled up on the chair.

Her eyes were closed as she let her hands feel the warmth of the cup. A slow breath was released from somewhere deep inside.

"Jesus," she whispered as her body began to relax.

Rabok and Salih were both with her still, and the Holy Spirit was moving in close.

"Why doesn't He just stay that close to her all of the time?" one of the newer angels asked.

"The human body could not handle it," Michael replied. "The presence of the Lord is so strong that humanity can only take such direct interactions in certain amounts."

The angel nodded.

"Plus, it would be difficult to stay grounded on earth with this much of heaven coursing through her being." Michael smiled as he continued, "And she needs to stay grounded so she can fulfill God's call on her life."

"How can she..." the angel started.

"Just a moment," Michael interrupted. "Allow the Holy Spirit to work."

A holy hush fell over the angelic band. All that was heard was the soft worship from Zral and Abei, and what sounded like a gentle brook flowing downstream.

The angelic beings knew this was coming from the living water flowing from the Holy Spirit to Cindy.

Cindy's chest rose and fell with a slow, steady rhythm. Her ears could not hear the stream, but her spirit could. She took it in.

She set down her coffee cup and laid her head on her knees. Rest was taking over her body. Not like the sleep she had earlier, but true rest.

The music coming from Zral and Abei had a gentle ebb and flow that matched the bubbling stream.

Kaleb and Hezek, along with Rabok and Salih, began to quote Scripture[2]:

"You who seek God, let your heart revive. For the Lord hears the needy and does not despise those of His who are prisoners. Heaven and earth shall praise Him, the seas and everything that moves in them."

The presence of the Holy Spirit began to spread out from Cindy. It stretched from the little kitchen table, past the counters and appliances, into the living room, and throughout the house.

Another holy hush fell on the angelic troops as they could sense the steady stream of the brook slowing down.

A few tears ran down Cindy's face as she sat up. She reached for a napkin from the table, wiped her eyes, and blew her nose.

"Thank You, Lord," she whispered.

She finished her coffee in time to hear her stomach growl. The clock revealed it was already mid-afternoon. She hadn't eaten yet, and it was clearly time.

Still in her robe, she made herself a peanut butter and jelly sandwich and wandered into the living room. It felt like her head was surrounded by thick cotton. Her mind was mostly quiet, but she still couldn't think about much.

Strange how time passes, she thought.

She scrolled through images and messages on her phone without really looking at anything in particular.

Oops. She scrolled back.

A friend from church had posted about the amazing service they had in the morning.

Oh no! We missed church!

Wait. What happened to Saturday?

Did I sleep for an entire day?

No.

No?

No.

With all of the fuss and anger and tears from the ladies' breakfast, Cindy hadn't even realized it was a completely different day!

Great! Angela is going to think we were mad about the party yesterday.

I still don't even know what happened!

Maybe she doesn't know it was weird.

Yeah, right, or maybe you cried like a baby in front of everyone for no reason!

Cindy cringed at the thought.

She had to call Angela and find out what happened. Surprised by her own braveness, she picked her phone up again, looked up Angela's number, and pressed "call" without so much as a second thought.

Her anxiety was building while she waited for Angela to answer.

"Hello?" It was her.

"Hello, Angela?"

"Yes! Is this Cindy?"

"It is."

"We missed you at church today. Are you feeling okay?"

Why did she ask that?

What does she know?

What happened yesterday?!

"Oh, I am feeling fine. Just a little tired." Cindy paused. "Listen, about yesterday," she said weakly.

"Oh, it was so wonderful to have you join us! Jackie and Bethany said they had a wonderful time chatting with you."

So far, so good.

"I'm sorry you had to leave early. Is everything okay with your parents?"

My parents? Why would she ask about my parents?

What happened! What did I say?

Just play it cool, Cindy.

"Oh, my parents? Yes, sure, they're okay."

"Okay, good. It sounded pretty urgent that you give them a call, so I'm glad everything is okay."

Cindy froze.

"We didn't know the details, but we prayed for you as soon as you left," Angela reported.

A call? Did I call them?

"Cindy, are you still there?"

"Oh yes. Yes. Listen, something just came up, and I need to go, but I will talk to you again later." She didn't wait for a goodbye or any such pleasantries. She just hung up and immediately switched over to her call history.

Thankfully, she rarely called anyone, so there wasn't much of a list.

There it was. The only call she made yesterday. "Mom and dad. 11:03 a.m."

How could you do that?

Cindy thought she should be angrier than she felt.

"The Holy Spirit finished His work in her," Salih observed. "Her denial regarding her parents is gone."

Then Cindy noticed that the call had only lasted three seconds. Not enough time to talk or even to leave a voice message.

As she set the phone down on the couch, an over-whelming sense of curiosity washed over her.

That was different, she thought to herself.

She decided to run with it.

"Okay, so I'm not angry anymore."

Self-talk started to feel a bit more natural, which was nice after hearing Mary recommend it for so many years.

"I know yesterday was really scary, and there is a big fight inside over what to do with the parents."

She chose her words carefully.

"I want to help. We all want the same thing."

I doubt that! someone retorted.

"No, really, I do," she continued. "We all want to be safe."

There was a moment of agreement internally. It was more of a sense than it was words. Cindy had never felt that before, and it felt good.

"We do. We all want to be safe," she repeated. "Let's see how we can do that."

Cindy was surprised she didn't even ask her parts about yesterday. Somehow, in this moment of unity, it just didn't seem important anymore.

Someone picked up the phone and dialed Mary.

Voicemail.

"Hi Mary, this is Cindy. I had quite the day yester-day. I will tell you about it Thursday. Well, if it's still important, I will. I mean, it's important, but things are happening. A lot of things are happening kind of fast. I think I realized something for the first time today." She paused. "We all want to be safe. That's what we all have in common. We all want to be safe." She smiled. "I thought you should know."

As she hung up the phone, she could hear more dialogue internally.

We may all want it, but it is impossible to agree on how to get it. It was the bitter, angry voice Cindy heard the most.

I am afraid we will make the wrong choice and have big consequences. It was the fearful voice that plagued her at the worst moments.

I want my mommy. This voice was accompanied by the soft crying Cindy had become accustomed to.

"I know you do." Cindy wasn't sure what to say. "We all wish our parents could have done a better job."

I don't. I hate them!

"Well, we all want to be around safe people."

Silence.

"We have to find out how. I think we can be safe. Maybe Mary can help."

I like her. The little one had stopped crying and was sniffling a bit.

"Me too. We will ask her on Thursday if she can help."
Cindy was feeling good about this little conversation. It
was the most she had ever had with her internal selves.

"Does anyone else want to say anything?"

All was quiet. The conversation seemed to have been
enough to calm everyone down.

Why have I never done that before? Cindy wondered as
she reveled in the silence. There was almost a sense of
peace inside—almost.

The rest of the evening passed without incident. Cindy was encouraged about her first day of work tomorrow. She knew it would be challenging, but she wanted
to do it more than ever. She ate a slightly healthier dinner than usual—macaroni and cheese with a little bit of
broccoli on the side—and headed to bed early.

"This isn't over yet," Michael warned. "She will sleep
good tonight thanks to the work of the Holy Spirit, but
there is still much to do."

Cindy's band of angelic beings took their posts
around the home. While she slept, they each worshipped the Lord in their own way.

Chapter 13

When morning came, Cindy awoke, refreshed and ready for the day. By 7 a.m., she had showered, eaten breakfast, and was sitting on the couch with her Bible in her lap. It was about thirty minutes before she had to leave for her first day at work, and she really wanted to read her Bible.

"Starting the day with the Word of God is always best," she said optimistically.

She stroked the Bible with her hand, hesitant to open it.

This never works, the angry part retorted.

"It will work today," Cindy replied confidently.

A few more strokes of the cover, and then she opened it. The pages fell open to Psalm 91[3].

She read: "He who dwells in the shelter of the Most High will rest in the shadow of the Almighty."

So far, so good.

"I will say of the Lord, 'He is my refuge and my fortress, my God, in whom I trust.'"

This isn't so bad. Cindy began to relax a bit.

"Surely He will save you from the fowler's snare and from the deadly…"

Her hand hit the cover hard as she slammed the book shut. She couldn't read it. Not that word, not any more words!

Sadness flooded her heart for a moment as she heard the sounds of crying and felt the pain of the moment.

"I'm so sorry," she whispered to herself. "I'm so sorry."

She sat on the couch for what was left of her thirty minutes, just staring at the floor. The day had been going so well! *I just wanted to start the day good for once,* she thought to herself. *Pull it together, Cindy. You have to get to work.*

At that, she pulled herself up from the couch, gathered her things, and headed to the car.

Is it just me, or do the days seem to be lasting longer?

Oh, well.

She slipped behind the wheel and started up her little blue Toyota. The car sputtered a little as the engine warmed up. The drive to work was nice.

If only all of life was nice like this.

Boring!

No, safe. That would be so safe.

Work isn't going to be safe.

It is just a job. Toughen up already!

It is more than a job. It is people, people everywhere!

Calm down. It will be fine.

Cindy listened to the banter inside for a while. Soon she pulled into the parking lot at the retail store where her new career would begin.

Career? You call this a career? This is so beneath you.

I have to be grateful for what I have.

This is all we can do right now. There is so much stress!

You shouldn't complain! Plenty of people have it worse than you.

Her head swirled with thoughts as she walked into the main door. For some reason, the swirling didn't bother her as much today.

"Hello, Cindy!" It was Mrs. Watson, there to meet her at the door. "You are so punctual, excellent!"

Cindy smiled as they shook hands.

"Follow me, please." Mrs. Watson headed to a register at the back of the store. "I will give you a short tour of the store and then get you started on training videos."

"Sounds good!"

"Of course, you will be working the sales floor. Mostly stocking displays and offering help to customers, but I wanted to get you familiar with the register area in case you need something."

Cindy nodded and listened intently as Mrs. Watson talked her through working the register and showed her the things behind the counter she might need to help a customer.

"That should do it. Any questions?"

"Not yet," Cindy responded.

"Okay, I'm sure questions will come up as we go." She turned to head to the back office. "Let's get you started on the training videos."

While Cindy was eager to start her new job, she was not eager to watch training videos, and they did not disappoint. Employees or actors, she wasn't sure which, filmed in the 1990s, talked her through the most mundane interactions and policies.

If a person needs to be trained in these things, they are idiots. Ah, Ms. Grumpy always had an opinion on things.

What if I forget what I am doing? What if I get fired! I have to listen very intently just in case.

Humph! You should talk to Mary about fear over here. She needs healing more than the rest of us!

Shut up! I'm not wrong.

I want to color. Cindy picked up a pen without thinking and started scribbling on a piece of paper from her bag.

Stop that! We have to be adults here.

Whimper.

When will these ridiculous videos be over!

It's a shame to do all of this boring work for a job we will lose anyway.

Finally, the training videos ended just in time. The voices were starting to wear Cindy out completely.

"Mrs. Watson?" she called as she peeked out from the training room.

"Mrs. Watson!" A voice down the hall echoed Cindy's.

Soon the professional and kind supervisor appeared in the hallway. "Did you finish up?"

"I sure did. What's next?"

"Well, I think that's all for today. Monday is one of our slowest times, so it won't do you much good to stick around."

"Okay," Cindy agreed.

"Tomorrow morning, we will start you working on the floor. You will train with Belinda. She is great and will show you everything you need to know."

"Wonderful! See you tomorrow!"

Cindy smiled as she walked out of the office area and onto the floor of the department store. It was a good first day. She stayed present—mostly—and she felt pretty good.

I think I'll walk around the store a bit to get the lay of the land, she thought to herself.

In the Shoe Department, a mom struggled to get new shoes on one of her two small children. Cindy smiled at the youngest playing in the stroller, oblivious to his surroundings, while his sister did all she could to not put on the new light-up shoes her mom so desperately was trying to get on her feet.

In Housewares, a young couple, possibly newly-weds, discussed what would make their new apartment perfect for when her mom visited next week.

As Cindy passed the magazines and books, a title caught her eye. It was a book on raising dalmatians. She thought about her conversation with Bethany and Jackie and how one of them would surely enjoy reading it.

Yes, but remember how that day ended? Oh, that's right, you can't!

That's just cruel, Cindy thought. Then the reality of the statement started to sink in. She really couldn't remember how it ended, and the very thought made her stomach sink.

"No, I'm not going to let that get me down!" she said just above a whisper. She pulled her chin up and spun around to leave the store.

In a flash, she was staring at her mother! She blinked. Sure enough. Her mother was standing just on the other side of the Ladies Clothing Department. It looked like she was shopping for skirts. Cindy was frozen.

Run! Run!

She couldn't.

Soft crying. *Mommy, mommy.*

Get out of here!

At that, her whole body jolted. She couldn't feel her legs moving, but the racks of clothes were flying by her, so she knew she must have been walking fast.

By the time she made it to the car, her face was stained with tears, and her body was trembling so much she couldn't get the keys out of her purse.

As she began to come back to her senses, she took an assessment of her location. She was in her little Toyota, parked between two SUVs. She had a fairly clear view of the door to the store, but she was far enough away that her mom wouldn't see her if she came out.

She let out a breath, and her body tried to relax. She took a few more deep breaths, then the tears came. Her whole body heaved as the tears flowed free. So many feelings!

Her face was buried in her hands as she leaned on the steering wheel. Tears were flowing freely, and she felt as if she might throw up.

I hate this! I hate them. I hate me. I hate everything!

There is no safe place! Nothing will ever be okay!

Why, oh, why did this happen!

While she was wailing her prayers to the Lord, Michael did a quick inventory of his guard. "Who is missing?" he asked after a quick headcount.

"James, one of the reinforcement troops," Hezek responded. "He was blocking the mother from seeing

Cindy. He must be staying in the store to keep watch until Cindy is able to leave."

"Very well," said Michael. "The rest of you be on the lookout. Darlene came out of nowhere, and I don't like surprises like that."

"Do you think this will set her back?" Salih asked.

"No, the Most High God does not have setbacks, and He is guiding this journey. He will undoubtedly use this to break down any remaining denial regarding her parents." Michael glanced over his shoulder. The Lord was still restraining the dark storm that had been revealed in the last session, but it was never far from them.

"This storm must be disconnected from her if she is ever to experience true freedom. We must continue to protect her while the Sovereign Lord breaks her free from denial. The Holy Spirit will strengthen her through the process."

The angels nearby nodded in agreement and took their positions near Cindy.

After ten minutes had passed, Cindy was weak but ready to head home.

So much for an uneventful first day.

This was so stupid!

Just shut up!

Her little Toyota slowly pulled into the driveway. Cindy had been quiet for the entire drive. She turned the car off and just sat there. It felt like it would take too much strength to walk inside, but she knew she had to.

After a few minutes of debating how long she could reasonably stay in the car, she pushed the car door open. It felt like a steel door as she pushed it and stepped out of the car. Her mind felt foggy and unclear as she stumbled into the house.

A trail of keys, wallet, purse, and shoes led from the door to her bed. She hit the bed face first and just laid there.

We can never go back.

We can never go out again.

Where was God?

Where was my protection?

Did He even know what was happening?

I am so done.

I am so done.

Cindy only woke up briefly that evening to call in sick to work. Mrs. Watson didn't answer the phone, and Cindy was relieved. She said she was ill and wouldn't make it tomorrow or Wednesday. She needed to see Mary before she could go back to work.

Angela had sent a text asking how her first day on the job went. Cindy didn't reply. She just went back to bed and slept—a deep, shut-out-the-world kind of sleep.

"The storm is growing," James reported to Michael. Michael moved to a nearby window to see for himself.

"The enemy knows he is close to defeat," Michael confirmed. "He will do anything he can to keep from getting disconnected from Cindy."

"I don't understand," one of the angels replied. "Why does he even want to be connected to her? Clearly, she is serving the Most High God now. That won't change. Why is the enemy fighting so hard?"

"This kind of battle is new to some of you," Michael said as he addressed his troops. "There is something to be learned here. The enemy cannot create life on his own. He cannot even create life to sustain himself. He must steal the life that God has placed in others. He steals it many ways, but one of the ways he takes it is to connect to humans through agreements and bonds made generationally."

His troops were listening intently.

"God is using the time here on earth to create an army for His kingdom, a royal priesthood of all who choose Him. Part of His design for building and training the future citizens of heaven is through generational inheritances." Michael glanced over to check on Cindy before continuing. "Attributes of faith, love, hope, and many others have been sent by the Holy Spirit into the bloodlines of each family. These giftings can grow and develop into powerful tools for the kingdom of God as the generations pass."

MORE THAN MEETS THE EYE

One more glance at Cindy revealed she was sleeping deeply. No demons in sight. Michael continued, "Of course, Satan wants to take advantage of this powerful pathway through the bloodlines. So, he steals, kills, and destroys his way in with generational curses. Once a generational agreement is made with Satan, a portal is connected to the bloodline. One by one, as generations fall into sin, the portal strengthens in size."

"But Cindy never chose the kind of sin that this storm brings. It is pure evil."

"No, but her parents did. And that sin was passed on to her through the horrific abuse that happened to her as a child. That, combined with the other abuse, forced her to make an agreement that she would not have made otherwise."

"So that's why this storm won't let go," James commented.

"Exactly. It was given permission to drain life force from Cindy slowly, and it has been doing that since she was a small child." Michael was solemn. "She must break the relationships with her parents to break the agreement with this storm."

The weight of the situation was heavy on Cindy's angelic guard. She was their charge, and the Most High God had given them great compassion for her.

"We have been dispatched to serve the Lord and support His purpose for Cindy. Now that God has revealed the storm, it is our job to follow our directive. Right now, that directive is to protect her in this area. We must stand strong and be alert." Michael's attention was drawn out the window as a bolt of lightning struck near the house. "The Lord will not restrain this storm forever, but He will restrain it long enough for Cindy to make a choice, her own choice, not a choice forced on her by others."

The others retook their posts. After a moment of silence, Zral and Abei began their song. They sang while Cindy slept.

Give thanks to the Lord, for he is good;
His love endures forever.
Let the redeemed of the Lord say this—
Those he redeemed from the hand of the foe,
Those he gathered from the lands,
From east and west, from north and south.[4]

For the next two days, the worshippers sang songs of the Most High God's great redemptive acts while Cindy slept. She barely moved from the bed to get a drink or go to the bathroom. She didn't eat. She didn't cry. She just slept.

Thursday morning arrived, and Cindy laid in bed, staring at the ceiling. She couldn't believe what day it was. The last few days were a blur. She remembered her first day at work—the good and the bad—but she didn't remember much else. She had hoped she had called into work to let them know she was ill because she didn't want to lose her job after one day. There was no way to know for sure, though.

Today was therapy, and she needed it! After a few more minutes of staring at the ceiling, she limped out of bed and into her closet. She pulled on a pair of jeans from the pile on the floor and a fresh t-shirt. Her shoes were a little harder to find, but soon she was in her car on the way to see Mary.

It had felt like weeks since she had seen her. There was desperation for therapy in her heart today, yet she also felt a deep dread, maybe even fear, about what would happen.

Oh, my stomach.

I'm hungry, said a little voice inside.

"I should probably get some breakfast," Cindy responded.

The drive-thru was short, and the breakfast burrito she ordered was terrible, but at least the coffee was hot. Hopefully, her stomach wouldn't growl too much during session.

As she arrived at the office and headed into the waiting room, Michael was already getting reports from his troops regarding the perimeter, the storm, and the office's interior. Everything was as expected, including the dark, growing storm outside that was attached to Cindy. The only thing that wasn't expected was the client who was seeing Mary before Cindy.

"Hello, Ronan, Gabe," Michael greeted them both as he entered Mary's office before Cindy to see for himself. He motioned to the client sitting across from Mary and commented, "This should be interesting."

Mary closed her notebook and took her glasses off as she closed her prayer, ending the session. "You did an excellent job today, Maggie. I think you are really beginning to hear the Lord in a new and powerful way. Do you want to schedule another session or just wait and see how things go?"

"Well," Maggie started, "I came in today thinking I would be fine without another session. Integration has been difficult but wonderful. Since all of my self-states have come together with me, I feel more stable and secure than ever! But for some reason, I feel like I should schedule one anyway. I'm not sure why."

"If you would like to, that is fine with me." Mary smiled and then brought out her calendar, and the two settled on a time to meet next Thursday. "This is my only opening for the next few weeks. I'm glad we were able to get you in!" Mary's smile always reflected the love of Jesus. Michael liked that about her.

"Thanks, Mary."

"You're welcome."

Maggie headed out the door and through the waiting room for the parking lot. As Maggie turned to open the door, she saw Cindy sitting in the lobby staring at her with her mouth ajar.

Maggie stopped for a moment and gave Cindy a sheepish smile. Then she turned and walked out of the building.

Cindy could not believe it.

She knew she wasn't supposed to ask about other clients, but she couldn't help herself. As soon as she saw Mary, she blurted out, "What was Mrs. Watson doing here?"

Chapter 14

Mary smiled and held the office door indicating Cindy should come in before they continue with the conversation. "Have a seat," she said in her usual pleasant demeanor.

"Thank you," Cindy said without thinking. "I know I am not supposed to ask about other clients, but I'm just, just, shocked."

Mary was quiet to let Cindy continue.

"Did you know she is my boss? At my new job. The one I just started. She is my boss! I know most of the clients you see are like me, well, kind of like me, and well, I just didn't expect..." Her voice trailed off.

Mary cleared her throat and answered as pleasantly as if she was talking about the coffee she had for breakfast. "Mrs. Watson did come out of my office, but it is wise not to assume why she was here."

Cindy's mind was still whirling.

"Remember, we talked about this when you initially came here?"

"I remember." Cindy still couldn't focus.

What was she doing here!

Is she like us? Does she have parts too?

Maybe she was spying on us! See, no one is safe!

She wasn't spying. That is stupid.

Then she does have parts!

We can't assume anything. Did you hear what Mary just said?

Soft crying.

"Cindy?" It was clear Mary had said her name more than once. "Are you still with me?"

"I'm here," Cindy said slowly as she tried to focus on Mary.

"I know your mind is probably whirling seeing your work-world collide with your therapy-world."

That's an understatement!

"Let's pray and see if the Lord can settle things down a bit."

Cindy nodded. It was all she could do as her thoughts, fears, and anxieties whirled in her mind.

"Father God," Mary began, "We welcome You into this place and into this time. I ask You to please silence any voices that are not of You."

Cindy's mind began to calm.

"Please remove anything of an evil spiritual nature from our surroundings and allow the Holy Spirit to settle in our midst."

Michael and his band made quick work of the pestering demons that were becoming visible in the room. "Thank You for giving us the opportunity to be in Your presence. Lead us in Your will and way today. In Jesus' name, we pray, amen." Mary glanced at Cindy. Her body was more relaxed, but she still sat with her eyes closed and her head bowed.

Mary busied herself with getting her notepad and pen ready. She took her glasses off and took a sip of water.

Cindy opened her eyes, took a deep breath, and lifted her head. "Thank you," she replied.

"Is that a little better?"

"Yes, it is. I still have a lot of thoughts about seeing Mrs. Watson here, but they don't seem to be running me over anymore." Cindy gave a sheepish grin as her eyes briefly met Mary's.

"Good." Mary gave a short, confident nod. "Where shall we begin today?"

"I'm not sure." Cindy started with her usual update about the week. She felt defeated over her job, and parts of her were afraid Mrs. Watson would fire her because she knew she was in counseling.

Mary talked her through her fears and offered some advice for work.

"But it doesn't seem like these are the things we should pray about," Cindy stated.

"I agree." Mary shifted in her chair. "Let's ask the Lord what He thinks."

Cindy agreed, and Mary began to pray, "Father God, thank You for helping Cindy to focus her thoughts and to sort through her feelings. You know what is important for us to talk about today, Lord. Please direct us."

The room was quiet for a moment, at least in the natural. Outside the office window, the dark storm that had been following Cindy around was raging. It was closer to the office than it had been the week before, and it was definitely more active.

"How are the troops holding up?" Michael asked.

"They are holding," Hezek responded. "The winds are intense, and slews of demons come with each gust, but we are holding our own."

Ronan approached Michael. "I have assigned my troops a stance closer to the office to keep the wily ones from breaking through." He glanced around the room, letting his eyes rest on the storm outside the window. "It's going to be a rough one today."

"Praise be to the Most High God," Michael responded.

"Praise be," Ronan said with authority in his voice.

"I think I see something," Cindy began. "It is the storm we saw last week."

"I thought we might start here," Mary commented. "What else?"

"Well, Jesus is standing between me and the storm. He has a large sword in His hand. He is smiling, but not in a playful sort of way." She thought for a moment. "I don't know how to describe it, actually. It's like He is waiting for something. Waiting for something He is really going to like."

"I see," Mary was taking notes as quickly as Cindy was talking. "Is He waiting on you for something?"

"Maybe." Cindy waited. "Yes, actually. He wants to know..."

Cindy was quiet, listening. Then she slowly opened her eyes and just sat staring at her lap.

Mary noticed the shift and stopped writing. She looked up at Cindy and paused before asking, "What did He say, Cindy?"

"You know what He said." Cindy didn't look up.

"Why don't you tell me."

Cindy searched the floor with her eyes and then spoke. "He told me I need to sever relationships with my parents." A single tear ran down her cheek.

By now, the demons were gushing from the storm cloud like a flood. A tall cosmic being had floated down from the darkness and was standing near the cloud, awaiting his moment to enter the small country office.

Ronan and Michael's troops were at full force. Swords and daggers clashed around the outside of the building. The power of the Sovereign God was holding back the evil from entering the office, but it was definitely fighting for ground outside of the office. "Its connection to Cindy is strong, but the Lord God is stronger!" Ronan declared.

"There is a lot of generational strength in this storm," Michael commented.

"Yes, there is." Ronan pointed to the portals flowing into the storm cloud from the top and behind. "You can see the connection points from her various ancestors."

"It will be a great victory to sever this darkness from her bloodline today!"

"Praise be to the Most High God!" both said in unison.

"Cindy, I know we have been working to this point for a while now," Mary started. "How do you feel about it?"

In her chair, Mary was relaxed. Ronan knew she could sense the battle outside. Her prayers had not stopped since Cindy walked into the room, but her demeanor was calm. He had served with her for many years. He admired her ability to remain at peace with a storm like this brewing just a few feet away. Her faith in the Lord grew with each victory, and the strength of his troops grew with her faith. She didn't need to see the storm or see the victory to know the Lord was working. This made serving the Most High God at her side an adventure that he and his troops enjoyed.

"I'm not sure." Cindy was staring at her hands. "I know the right answer, but I just don't know what to say."

"What do you hear from your heart? What are your parts saying?"

"Lots of things, really."

"Why don't you listen internally and tell me what you hear."

"Okay."

Cindy listened for a few minutes.

What are we doing! This is a terrible idea!

The little one was crying again, or still. Cindy was never sure.

I just want this to be over. It is so scary.

God can do this for us. We just have to believe!

Cindy reported each of the thoughts to Mary. "It just keeps cycling around and around," she explained. "It never stops, really. Someone is afraid of doing this, actually. She is always afraid of everything."

Cindy listened again.

"Then there is the angry girl. She carries so much weight. Sometimes, I can see an image of her. Her face is twisted, and she is always mad about something. She is mad about all the parents did to us... um... to me, and she wants to do terrible things! Sometimes, I can't bear to listen to her."

Cindy paused. "Then there is the little one. You've talked to her before. She is so small and afraid. She cries a lot. She wants my mom to be her mommy. She can hardly stand the thought of giving up on that dream."

So stupid!

"She just wants to be taken care of." Cindy stopped.

"Anyone else?" Mary inquired.

"Well, yes, there is a part that is always insulting me. It calls me 'stupid' and other things. For a long time, I thought it was the angry girl, but lately, I have been thinking it is another part."

"Why is that?"

"Well, that voice just feels a little different. I think everyone else just wants to be free of my parents, even the little one. She knows mom will never be a 'mommy' to us. It just makes her sad. But this voice is different."

"Different how?"

Don't tell her. She'll never understand.

Just another person thinking you are crazy. Yeah, that's what you need!

Thoughts of recent encounters with Angela began to come to Cindy's mind. How foolish she felt running out of the coffeehouse. And the breakfast at Angela's on Saturday? Wow, that was bad.

You don't even know what you did!

I know it was terrible.

You can't remember because it was so bad. You would be horrified.

Cindy's mind whirled with thoughts of what might have happened that day. She had no memory of it—none. So, she could fill in endless details of what could have been, and none of them were good.

"She's spiraling," Michael observed.

"What do we do?" Gabe asked with his sword drawn.

"Just wait," Ronan answered. "Mary will notice, the Lord will reveal the demon, and we will take care of him."

Mary did notice. "Father God, please silence every voice that is not of You."

At her request, the demon could no longer hide. The instant he appeared, a sword banished him from the room.

Cindy let out a long breath. Her shoulders slumped.

"Is that better?" Mary asked.

"Yes." Cindy struggled for words. "How did you know to pray that?"

"Cindy, there is a battle going on, a battle for you, a battle for each of us. The Lord has given us all of the tools to walk in victory. We just have to know to use them." She paused to allow her words to sink in. "I know you have a lot of internal voices that keep your mind pretty crowded. Your enemy knows this too. Sometimes he blends in with the other voices to amp up your fear, anxiety, worry, whatever. When that happens, you spiral faster and deeper." She paused again to make sure Cindy was tracking with her. "Thankfully, the Lord has given us authority over these voices. They are not of Him, and they are not of us. When we take authority over them, they must leave."

Cindy nodded. "The difference is big."

"Yes, it is," Mary agreed. "God is fighting for you. We will do what He wants today. Agreed?"

A small smile came across Cindy's face. "Agreed."

"So, let's talk about this boundary with your parents."

Cindy talked about the abuse memories that had come to mind over the past week. They were terrible—filled with pain and sadness but mostly filled with loneliness. A few times, Mary prayed and asked the Lord to bring peace to specific memories, but she mostly let Cindy process her thoughts and feelings. There were a few not-bad memories with her parents, but even those were tainted with manipulation and evil agendas.

The tears were flowing freely now, and Mary knew Cindy was almost ready.

"It sounds like you are ready to ask the Lord to disconnect you completely from your parents and to cleanse your bloodline of this massive storm of evil."

"I am," Cindy agreed. "I am willing to give up my hopes and dreams of having the happy family I always wanted. I know they will never be that."

"You don't have to give up on that dream, Cindy. We just need to separate that dream from your biological family."

Cindy's head tilted with interest.

"You see," Mary continued, "God has a plan of hope for you. He wants your future to be good. You can put your hopes and dreams in the Lord."

"I'm not sure what to hope for."

"That will come with time, but first, let's take care of this storm, okay?" Mary smiled reassuringly.

Cindy agreed and closed her eyes to pray.

"This is it," Ronan announced.

The two troops of angels were already alert, but now they could feel the Holy Spirit settling in the room stronger than before. As Mary prayed, their swords glowed with the power of the Most High God.

"It is time," Hezek said as he and Kaleb moved closer to Cindy with swords drawn.

As the glow intensified, so did the storm. "Look!" Abei shouted, pointing to the sky.

They all looked up. A ball of holy fire was coming from heaven. It was headed directly at the office, straight for Cindy. Zral, Abei, and the other worshippers lifted their voices, the warriors all lifted their swords, and Rabok and Salih took hands encircling Cindy and bracing for impact.

As Mary and Cindy ended their lengthy prayer renouncing the powerful strongholds Cindy's parents had over her life, the fireball hit with a fury! It produced a nuclear-sized cloud that encompassed all of the demons, the dark storm cloud, and even the tall cosmic being. In an instant, it was all gone—completely consumed by the power of the Most High God.

Cindy and Mary both felt it as well. As the fireball hit the space, Cindy felt a rush of cool water wash over her entire being. The space around her felt empty. For the first time ever, there was no open portal, no darkness trying to invade her life. She was free.

The angels raised their swords to the heavens and shouted in victory.

"Did you feel that?" Cindy asked in awe, trying to process what she was feeling.

Mary's smile was reflecting the glory of God that had consumed the office. "God has been fighting for you since day one, but today, you have felt the strength of His fight!" Mary declared.

"I did. I really did." Cindy didn't have words for what she had just experienced.

The two sat in silence for a moment. Breathless and speechless from what had just happened.

"If only they could hear the celebration!" Gabe exclaimed.

"Praise be to the Most High God!"

"Praise be to the Most High!"

"Praise be to the Most High!"

The angelic bands were worshipping and praising the Lord throughout the office and across the property. Glory shined down from heaven, and they could hear the angels around the throne of God celebrating along with them.

Meanwhile, in the space around them, Cindy was still trying to process what had just happened.

"So, what does this mean?" Cindy asked.

"Everything is different now," Mary explained. "Your parents only have the power you give them now. They can no longer control you spiritually or otherwise."

"But how is this different from all of the other prayers, renunciations, forgiveness, all of the things we have been doing for years now? How do I know that anything is really different?"

"Let's ask Jesus about this. He has been your advocate through this whole healing journey; He can answer your questions."

Cindy agreed again, and they both bowed their heads and closed their eyes.

"Father God, Jesus Christ, and Holy Spirit, can You please help Cindy understand what is different now."

Almost immediately, a picture started forming in Cindy's mind.

"I see the massive storm cloud from earlier. It is rematerializing, almost like someone rewinding a video." She paused. "Except this video is going farther back than just the beginning of the session. It is going back years and even decades."

"This is important. Watch closely," Mary encouraged.

The two were quiet for a moment, and then Cindy opened her eyes. "Wow, that was amazing."

"What did Jesus show you?"

"He took me back in time. The storm cloud that looked so massive today was much larger when I started my healing journey. Back then, there was hail, many tornadoes, and the lightning strikes were directly impacting my life. He showed me that throughout my healing and all of the prayers we have done, the storm has been losing power. Each prayer, each renunciation took away some of its ability to impact me and pulled it farther away from me."

"That's amazing." Mary smiled.

"But there was more." Cindy paused. "He showed me the storm when I was born. It was strong then, about the size it was today. It came for me at conception because of the generational inheritances passed through my parents' bloodline, but it grew more and more with each act of abuse in my childhood." Cindy sat in silence as she processed what she was saying. "Up until this point, today, we have been disconnecting all of the evil attached during my lifetime, but today, God dealt with the evil that attached at conception."

The room was quiet.

"I can't believe it." Cindy was still trying to process the enormity of what the Lord had done. It seemed too much to comprehend in the minutes they had left of session. "What do I do now?"

"Now," Mary began, "I think you will be able to honor those boundaries with your parents that we set."

"I think I will. I want to now. I mean, I wanted to before, but now I feel like I can. And I want to."

They both smiled.

Mary said a wrap-up prayer and closed up the session.

As Cindy walked out the door, her band of angelic supporters followed her out. When Mary had prayed the Lord would protect Cindy from any retaliation for what He had done in session, the warriors in the parking lot had to make quick work of a group of demons hanging around her car.

"The drive home should be smooth," Michael told the others. And it was.

Cindy's mind was relatively quiet for all that had happened in session. She was surprised. She thought there would have been more blowback for what she had done, what they had done.

She could hear the little one crying from time to time, and she knew the others were having hushed conversations between them.

Cindy rolled her window down and let the breeze blow through her hair as she drove. "It feels like it's just me here," she thought to herself. "I have never felt this before."

We are still here.

She heard the reply. She didn't mind.

"I know you are. I mean, it is just me, just us."

The darkness is gone.

"I think it is." Cindy pushed play on her CD and listened to her favorite worship music the rest of the drive. This was something she could rarely do because of the battle inside. Today was different.

As she drove, she began to notice the area where she lived for the first time. The town was small, quaint. The town square was composed of a dozen or so small boutiques and bakeries with an impressively landscaped city hall sitting in the middle. Just past the stores was a cozy little neighborhood filled with homes of every different color and size. Most of them had been there for decades.

Her house was on the outskirts of town. She decided to drive for a bit before heading straight home. The song she was listening to was praising God's goodness and His grace. She thought about that word: grace.

"God of grace," she said out loud. "God of grace," she repeated, letting it sink into her mind and heart.

She thought of all of the healing she had received over the years. For the first time, she could really see it. Despite how messy she still felt, she could see the changes in her heart and mind.

"I did nothing for this," she said to no one in particular.

So many times, she had wanted to pray or read her Bible, and she just couldn't. Parts of her were resistant, or she would try and get triggered. She wanted to worship, go to a small group, and be involved at church. She wanted to tell people about the Lord, but she just couldn't. There was some kind of internal block that kept her from serving the Lord the way she desperately wanted.

She drove past a small gas station and decided she should turn around and head home.

None of the healing journey had been earned. "None of it," she whispered.

She turned the music up a little louder and replayed Track number eight, "Grace." It's all God's grace.

For the rest of the drive, she felt comforted in the realization of God's grace in her life. It was an entirely new feeling, and she liked it. It was so different to feel God's presence in her life through the lens of grace.

When Cindy got home, her house even felt different. Like it was truly hers for the first time. So strange.

There is still tomorrow, she heard a voice say.

Cindy moaned. She had forgotten all about work and Mrs. Watson. What was she going to do?

We have to go to work. We have already missed so many days, and we need this job!

Cindy could feel her peace slipping away.

I'm so scared! What if she fires us!

That's illegal. She can't fire us for seeing a therapist.

She knows we can't have a lawyer. We are broke. Of course, she could fire us!

"God's grace," Cindy whispered, trying to remind herself of her thoughts on the drive home.

Stop it! You are scaring the little one.

Shut up, all of you!

Cindy found herself curled up on the couch with her soft green blanket wrapped around her shoulders. She didn't remember getting it, but obviously, she did. Clearly, tomorrow was still an issue. "How can God do such a big work, and I still be bothered by the everyday details of life?"

Duh, you just need more faith!

You are a stupid idiot, and you will never be better than this!

"Hold up." Cindy froze. "That didn't sound like me." She sat up a little straighter. "Jesus, please make any voices that are not of You or me be quiet, in Jesus' name!"

Whop! A sword split through three demons that just appeared in the room.

Cindy relaxed a bit, thankful that Mary had taught her about the "extra voices" that can try to slip into her system.

A sense of gratitude washed over her for just a second then it was gone.

Tomorrow. How do I handle tomorrow?

Chapter 15

Tomorrow came sooner than expected. Cindy was still asleep on the couch, wrapped in her green blanket, when her phone alarm went off. Startled, she grabbed it and slapped around on the front of it until the music finally stopped.

She laid back down and pulled the blanket over her head. What a week! The TV remote was next to her, and a few snacks were lying on the floor. This was nothing new. Cindy was used to waking up to debris surrounding her that she had no memory of creating.

"Lord, I have no idea how today is going to work out. Please be with me. Please help me with Mrs. Watson. You know I need this job."

After a few moments of wishing she didn't have to get up, she decided she should move, or she would have even more regrets. There was no time for her morning coffee at her favorite spot in the kitchen; there was barely enough time for a quick shower and a fresh change of clothes.

One look in the mirror and dread washed over her again. Somehow the dread was mixed with hope, such a strange combination of emotions. She turned to check her full view in the mirror. Her navy blue suit was slightly out of style. Five or six years ago, she had needed a new outfit for a big meeting in San Diego. She could remember shopping all day long until she came upon this nicely tailored navy dress suit. It fit her perfectly back then. Today, it was good enough. She did one last check of her hair and makeup and headed to the car.

I'm so nervous, but a little excited too.

Today is going to be terrible! I am going to get fired for sure!

I don't want to see Mrs. Watson! I'm so scared!

Whatever happens, happens. God is with us no matter what.

Sure, you say that now, but what about when Mrs. Watson calls us out in front of everyone for seeing a therapist.

Remember, she was at Mary's office too.

Yeah, but we have no idea why. She could have been talking about us!

That's ridiculous!

The little one was crying again. Not quite as loud as usual, but still crying.

Cindy was about to get into the car. Where were her keys?

Did I leave them inside?

Where are they?

This is ridiculous! You can't even keep track of your keys! How can you possibly keep a job!

Shut up! Just shut up!

She sighed and headed back into the house.

Not by the door, not in the kitchen, not in the living room, wait!

By the couch! Of course, that's where I collapsed when I got home last night.

Let's give this one more try!

This time, she made it all the way to work. She didn't remember the drive, but she was relieved to be there, sort of.

Michael had already sent angels ahead to scout out the store and the surrounding parking lot. All clear. Mrs. Watson was in her office. This time, Michael's scout reported quite a crew of angels with Mrs. Watson.

Cindy was sitting in her car, trying to work up the courage to head into the store.

After a few minutes, she determined she was going in no matter what! She just needed to get this over with, one way or another.

She walked at a quick pace from her car to the store. A brief pause before opening the door, a deep breath, and a whispered prayer, and she was ready. The door was heavy as she pulled it open and walked through. It felt like a major accomplishment which she instantly felt stupid for feeling.

As she glanced around, she noticed a few customers in the jewelry department, an employee at the open register, and Mrs. Watson at the back of the women's department.

Cindy started to duck past the women's clothing and head to the back office to check in, but too late! Mrs. Watson saw her!

"Cindy!" she called as she made her way to the aisle. "Good morning! May I speak to you for a minute?"

Cindy groaned to herself.

"Sure, Mrs. Watson." She followed her through the office doors and into Mrs. Watson's office.

"Have a seat, Cindy. I just wanted to talk to you about something."

Cindy sat down. Her entourage of angelic beings filled the room, mingling with Mrs. Watson's angelic beings. All seemed content. The room was peaceful, and clearly, the Holy Spirit was present.

Cindy noticed the nameplate on Mrs. Watson's desk: Maggie Watson.

Maggie seems like a nice name.

Nice or not, you are about to get fired.

Whatever! Who cares, even! I never liked this job anyways.

You need this job!

Cindy dismissively brushed her hair out of her face, forgetting for a moment that it was all pulled back in a bun.

"I just wanted to talk about seeing each other at Mary's office last Thursday."

Here it comes.

"I thought that was you." The words sounded even more fake than they felt.

Of course, you knew it was her.

Maggie smiled. "Well, it was me. I know there are a lot of confidential things that happen there, but I asked Mary if it would be okay if I told you why I was there."

Okay, that's not what I was expecting.

"She thought that would be fine." Maggie paused and then continued, "I won't ask why you were there, and, in case you were wondering, Mary didn't tell me anything about you." She smiled warmly.

Cindy shifted in her chair. She was glad she didn't have to talk about herself, but somehow it didn't seem any less awkward.

"Anyway, I wouldn't normally have this conversation with an employee, but Mary thought it would be okay, and I feel good about it. I won't go into any detail, but since you saw me at my counselor's office, I thought it would be better just to be honest, so you didn't have to wonder."

The heavenly beings saw a holy glow began to fill the office. They knew the Lord was in what was about to happen. Michael recognized at that moment that God had arranged for Maggie and Cindy to pass that day for a purpose. He didn't know what that purpose was yet, but he knew it would be good.

"Let's surround her with some support," Michael directed. Rabok and Salih took the cue and moved in close to Cindy. The Holy Spirit began to settle around her. She shifted once more and then relaxed into her chair.

"I had a lot of problems when I was a child. Well, I guess I didn't have problems, the adults in my life had problems, and I, well, I suffered the consequences of their problems." She waited to see how Cindy was taking in the information. "Are you okay with this so far?"

Cindy nodded. She wasn't sure if she was okay or not, but the nod happened, so she went with it.

Maggie continued, "It wasn't until well into adulthood that I realized how bad the consequences of my childhood really were." Her eyes looked around the room as if trying to find the next words.

For a moment, only the sound of the worshipping angels could be heard in the room.

"Well, I realized I couldn't function. What I had thought was functioning was really just poor coping. Don't get me wrong. I am so very thankful for the coping systems I had. I would not have survived childhood without them, but they couldn't provide the level of functioning that I wanted or needed as an adult."

Cindy didn't move. She could relate to every word she was hearing.

"So, God brought me to Mary." Maggie smiled, gazing off into the distance. "Finding her was the miracle I was praying for. She helped me accept my terrible childhood—and my coping system—and she helped me connect better to the Lord. I was able to heal in a way I never knew was possible." Her eyes settled on Cindy. "Do you know Jesus, Cindy? I know that is a little forward for a supervisor to ask, but since you were at Mary's, I think you must be a believer as well."

"I am," was all Cindy could say.

"Wonderful! Well, Jesus is the one who saved me. He didn't just give me salvation, but He saved me from what would have been a marginal life at best." The room fell quiet again. "I don't know what your struggle is, and I know I am your boss, but I want you to know I am praying for you. I pray for all of my employees, actually, but I feel a special burden to pray for you. I have since the day I met you."

Cindy didn't know what to say.

Although Cindy and Mrs. Watson couldn't see it, the room was filled with light from heaven. The Holy Spirit had settled in their midst, and the worshipping angels were all singing praises to the Most High God. Something divine was happening in that office, something that didn't happen every day.

"This meeting is directly connected with God's war strategy," Michael commented to no one in particular.

"His war strategy?" a ministering angel responded.

"Yes, God has a war strategy for bringing all of His children into the kingdom of God. Everything He does is to that end, but sometimes we can witness an act that is directly connected to that war strategy." Michael smiled. "This is one of those moments."

The angels nodded as they looked around the room. It was something to see the presence of the Lord in this way. They wondered if Maggie or Cindy could feel it.

"That's really all I wanted to say, Cindy. Do you have any questions for me?"

"No. Thank you for telling me." Cindy had no more words. Her mind was whirling, though, and it was making it hard for her to stay in the conversation.

"I know this was a lot to take in, and if you need to take an hour or so, or even the rest of the day to process it, I completely understand."

There was that welcoming smile again. Something about Mrs. Watson reminded Cindy a bit of Angela.

Why would she offer to let us go home for the day? So, what if she is in counseling! What do I care?

You know we can't focus, we can't even think!

The little one was whimpering.

This is so, so scary!

Sheez. You baby!

Why do I feel so angry about this!

I need this job!

She just gave us permission to go home.

I can't go home. What will she think?

Cindy didn't say a word but stood up to walk to the door. She wobbled and grabbed the chair for balance. She didn't want to look to see if Mrs. Watson had noticed.

Of course, she noticed, she is four feet away.

Dumb, dumb, dumb.

Just get out of here!

Cindy focused on her feet and then on the door. As she regained her balance, she walked to the door, turned to Mrs. Watson, and paused for just a moment. "Thanks," was all she could think to say.

Is she like me? Does she have parts?

Can she see my parts? Does she know I have all of these different self-images?

What does this mean for me?

What does this mean for my job?

Her head was spinning on the drive home—so many thoughts, so many thoughts. She couldn't pick out one in particular. They all seemed smashed together somehow. Her stomach was churning, but she didn't know why.

Did I eat breakfast? she wondered.

The house seemed loud, but she knew it was her own mind.

Usually, her bed was warm and comfortable. Right now, she couldn't even feel it. Somehow, she knew she still had her work clothes and even her shoes on, but she didn't know it enough even to care. She drifted off to sleep.

Saturday was a blur. She had sent several texts to Mary giving her updates on work and her internal thoughts. It seemed as if everything was getting more and more jumbled in her mind.

Sunday morning, Cindy decided she was brave enough to try church. In her heart, she hoped the change of scenery would help her feel more grounded and more like herself. She had been so disoriented since her meeting with Mrs. Watson, and she just needed a sense of her own normal again.

"It is so dumb to be thrown off by something so ridiculous!" she whined as she got ready to leave.

Sitting in the parking lot outside the church, she checked her makeup one more time. She couldn't focus. She felt herself get out of the car and head into the main entrance.

The smell of the church helped a bit. It was an older building, and there were arrangements of fake flowers and trees in the lobby. A tiny bit of a musty smell was always present. One deep breath later, and she began to feel herself coming back. She settled into her usual spot, three rows from the back on the end, and waited for church to begin.

She liked it here, most of the time. Sitting three rows from the back didn't make it look like she was ready to bolt at any moment—even though she was—and the end seat gave her the view of most of the people in front of her. She had attended this little country church for the past five years. Most people had come to know her as the quiet girl that sat three rows from the back on the end, and aside from a few polite greetings, most people let her be. Most people, except Angela, of course! And there she was, headed right for Cindy.

"Good morning, Cindy!"

Cindy stood, a bit on auto-pilot, knowing a hug was inbound.

She hated those hugs, and yet she craved them deeply.

"How are you today?"

"I'm okay, I guess."

"How is the new job?" Angela still had her hand on Cindy's arm in a friendly sort of way.

"Um... it has been difficult," was all she could find to say.

"New jobs can be hard," Angela affirmed. "I'll have to stop by and visit someday when you are working."

Cindy knew she offered that as a comfort, but it just felt a bit too intrusive.

"That's okay. I think that would be strange." Her hand flew to her mouth. Had she just said that out loud?

Angela didn't seem offended. "Oh, I could see that. No worries, we can just grab coffee again sometime."

Before Cindy could say more, Jackie and Bethany had joined them.

"Cindy! We missed you last week!" Bethany was so smiley. Cindy shifted her weight from one leg to the other, letting Angela's hand drop away from her arm.

"Oh, well, I had a few things going on," Cindy stammered.

"It's no problem," Jackie piped in. "We just wanted to let you know you were missed." She gave Cindy an awkward side hug and waved goodbye as she and Bethany headed to their seats.

"I know it may not always feel like it, but you really are part of our family here, Cindy." Cindy let Angela gaze into her eyes for a second longer than usual before she looked away.

Part of our family.

"You don't need to say anything," Angela squeezed her arm gently and then turned to go. She paused for a moment and turned back to Cindy.

A tall, broad-shouldered angel was standing behind Angela. He had a kind look on his face, and Michael recognized him as a messenger angel sent from the Lord to make sure important information was communicated.

"I thought you should know," Angela began, "we had planned to have the worship service next month at Sutton Place."

Cindy's stomach turned.

"Anyway, we prayed about it the day of the ladies' breakfast, and we really felt like it wasn't the right place for us. So, we are still looking for a place to host. I just thought you should know." Angela smiled one more time. She didn't wait for a response this time, just turned and headed to the front row where she sat each weekend for service. As she left, the messenger angel was gone.

Cindy blinked a few times. Still standing by her seat, she wasn't sure what had just happened.

The Lord did it.

He did it.

God spoke and set a boundary for me.

"God's grace," she said to herself.

Cindy felt a shiver. She instinctually rubbed her arms and took a seat. She couldn't believe the Lord did that.

A sense of protection and safety passed over her, covering her entire being like a warm blanket.

God loves me. God loves me.

As the pastor opened the service and the music began to play, Cindy sat in her chair, letting her thoughts flow freely. A single tear rolled down her face. She had a new sense of what God's protection would be like. She remembered Him removing the storm of her parents' control in the last session, and now He was speaking to other people to keep her safe. She could hardly believe it.

No more mommy? the little one wanted to know.

Angela's words began to roam through Cindy's mind: *Part of our family. Part of our family.* The words felt foreign. She wanted them to be true, but she was so afraid.

Maybe this is what Mary meant by keeping my hope for the future. Maybe God does have a family for me, just not the kind I was expecting.

Cindy wasn't sure what to think, but the warm protection she felt all around made it safe to think about it.

Rabok and Salih were close to her, and the Holy Spirit had settled on her.

Zral and Abei were singing with the church's worship team, lifting praises to the Lord.

Cindy let the music flow through to her heart. It was nice. She could feel the Lord's presence. She closed her eyes and just sat. She sat in His presence and let her mind do whatever it wanted.

"Jesus, be with me," she prayed. Mary had taught her the importance of inviting the Lord into her thoughts instead of trying to push them away to get to Him.

Throughout the church, angels were worshipping the Most High God. As the people's hands were raised, the angels' voices became louder, and their weapons' glow increased.

"Worship brings victory," Michael stated. "As these people worship the Lord, victories are taking place all over the world—for people they are praying for, situations that need the Lord's intervention. So many things are happening!"

"Praise be to the Most High God!" Michael's troops shouted.

"Praise be to the Most High," Michael echoed. He looked at Cindy. Her eyes were closed, and to someone nearby, she might have looked asleep, but he knew otherwise.

Soon more tears began to fall down her face. She didn't make a sound, she didn't move, but the tears flowed.

"Praise be to the Most High God," Michael almost whispered the words as he watched with reverence as the Holy Spirit worked in Cindy's heart.

When the music ended, the intensity of the Holy Spirit's presence lifted. Someone had placed a Kleenex box near Cindy on the pew. When she opened her eyes, she was a little embarrassed when she saw it, but she experienced a bit of gratitude.

The pastor began his sermon as Cindy finished blowing her nose as silently as possible. Salih was still nearby, helping her to experience her emotions and sit with them in peace. She took out a notepad and began to write down some of her thoughts.

I don't understand everything that is happening to me. I want to believe that the Lord is working to heal me. I want to believe that, one day, things will be better, but it is so hard to hope. It is terrifying. What if nothing changes? What if I go through all of this and nothing is different? But I see a difference, I feel a difference, so I know things are changing. I don't want to be the same Cindy I have always been. I want to be who God made me to be. I just don't know if that is possible. I don't even know where to fight anymore or who to fight. I'm just so tired.

"Her faith is strong," Michael observed.

"But her words express doubt and fear," James questioned.

"True, but her heart of faith allowed her to write these words. It's her faith that allows her to express her fears and doubts. Her faith keeps her strong." A small smile came across Michael's face. "One day soon, she will discover her faith, and I believe she will find the next battle to fight."

The service ended, and Angela glanced back. Cindy was no longer there.

Chapter 16

Monday morning came as usual. Cindy's bed was more comfortable than usual. Her workday awaited her, and she still wasn't sure how to respond to Mrs. Watson. As she showered and dressed, she determined she needed the job. Mary knew both her and Mrs. Watson, and she didn't seem concerned about the two working together, so she just needed to toughen up and deal with it.

She set her empty coffee cup in the sink, grabbed her purse and keys, and headed to the door.

When she arrived at work, she was surprised to see the place already busy with customers. She hadn't had much training yet and wasn't sure what she would be doing. Thankfully, a young lady with long brown hair and a pretty smile greeted her as she walked toward the back office.

"Cindy?"

"Yes, that's me."

"Hi! My name is Amanda." She put her hand out, and Cindy shook it. "Mrs. Watson asked me to train you on customer service today."

Oh, good, we don't have to deal with Mrs. Watson.

At least not yet.

"Thank you. I was wondering how today was going to go." Cindy forced a smile.

Amanda returned her smile and headed toward the Women's Department. "Follow me, please. I will start by showing you through some of the departments and signage we have up."

"You probably know most of this already because you shop here, but today I want to show you the store from the owner's perspective, not the shopper."

Cindy nodded. For some reason, that intrigued her.

"You see, the customer just sees the surface. They see what they are looking for or what they expect from a store. But the owner has to see more than that. The owner is always anticipating needs and arranging things to make it easier for the customer. Mrs. Watson is changing the way retail works in this area by teaching these strategies at every employee level, not just those in marketing. She believes as we become more educated behind the why of what we do, we will do it better!"

"That makes sense." Cindy's hand nonchalantly passed over a rack of sweaters.

"Like that, for example," Amanda began as she pointed to Cindy touching the sweaters. "Owners know that people like to engage their senses in their shopping experience. So, they want to create a store that is full of experiences and not just products. What do you notice with your senses?"

Cindy paused. "Well, I hear music playing. The store smells wonderful. I love how these sweaters feel." She smiled as she touched them again.

"Good, good. But there is so much more!" Amanda motioned all around her. "If you do it right, customers don't notice what you have done, but they do experience it." She pointed to the walls and ceiling. "From the color on the walls to the light fixtures, even the air conditioning ducts, it is all designed so that customers feel comfortable, so they feel welcome."

"I never thought of that before," Cindy mused.

"Most people don't. They aren't supposed to. But we are." Amanda picked up an empty coffee cup someone had left on a shelf. "Like this, for example. If you go into a store with trash, what do you think?"

"That the store isn't well-maintained."

"Of course! That's what most people would think! I can guarantee you as floor manager that this store is very well maintained. But our customers are still human—so are our employees for that matter—so sometimes there is trash, or a broken display, or a line of products that don't meet expectations. Our job is not to police each customer that comes in the store, but rather to make every person feel welcome and try to anticipate their needs."

Cindy nodded. She was beginning to understand. "So, you want me to see the bigger picture. The purpose behind what we do and how we do it."

"Yes. Mrs. Watson believes that how we view our customers and each other is very important. She wants this store to be a safe place for each person who comes in."

"Anticipating customer needs and giving the benefit of the doubt, that sort of thing," Cindy replied. *Like God's grace*, she thought briefly.

"Exactly!" Amanda smiled. "Now, of course, if someone were shoplifting or intentionally hurting another person, we would take action and call the police if needed, but that training is not for today." She smiled again. "Now, let's go over the bigger picture of store management."

Amanda walked Cindy through the store policies, store design, and employee manual. Never before had Cindy had a training experiencing quite like this one. After Amanda adjusted her perspective to see the bigger picture, the most mundane aspects of training, like the employee handbook, suddenly held greater meaning and, consequently, greater interest. It was like she saw everything from behind the scenes instead of just another process to get through.

Amanda asked how her first day of training had gone.

"It was fascinating," Cindy replied.

"That's what I was hoping for!" Amanda beamed with pride as her student seemed to be grasping the bigger picture of working in retail.

"I see from the calendar that you are off work tomorrow. So, we will continue your training on Wednesday."

"Sounds good!" Cindy said, and she meant it.

On the drive home, Cindy was lightly drumming her steering wheel with her thumbs to the beat of one of the songs playing at work.

It wasn't until she was settled on the couch in her favorite sweatpants and t-shirt with her dinner in hand that she realized how quiet her mind had been all day.

"Is anyone there?" she questioned.

Silence.

"Interesting," she said just under her breath.

Oh, we're still here.

Today was not as scary as I thought.

The little one was sniffling more than crying today.

We dodged Mrs. Watson for one day, but what about Wednesday?

"I don't know. She doesn't seem as intimidating to me now for some reason." Her first bite of dinner hung mid-air on her fork as she thought about that for a moment. "I'm not sure why, though." After another thought, she shrugged and pushed the fork into her mouth with one hand while grabbing the remote with the other. She clicked on the TV and let the sounds fill the room.

Thoughts of the day flowed through her mind. There was some conversation about this or that between the parts. She just let it all be. She felt content.

"This is a new feeling," she said out loud.

Michael was looking up at something. "This should be good!" he said with a smile.

The angels around him followed his gaze. Descending from heaven was a cloud the size of a man's fist.

Rabok and Salih recognized what was happening. They knew the Holy Spirit was coming in a new and different way tonight. They gathered around Cindy to prepare the way for the Spirit of God to rest on her.

"What is going to happen?" Zral asked.

"I don't know." Michael stroked his chin. "Whatever it is, I believe it is a continuation of the last few weeks. It seems we are entering into a new level of healing for Cindy." He turned his attention toward Kaleb and Hezek, "Let's stay alert in case there is resistance." His voice was calm and filled with peace.

"Yes, sir!" the angels responded, each taking their position.

Worship began to rise from the worshipping angels:

There is a river whose streams make the city of God happy,
The holy dwelling places of the Most High.
God is in the midst of her; she will not be moved;
God will help her when morning dawns.
The nations made an uproar the kingdoms tottered;
He raised His voice, the earth quaked.
The cloud settled on Cindy's heart connecting with the Holy Spirit dwelling in her. It was beautiful to see.
The Lord of armies is with us;
The God of Jacob is our stronghold.
Come, behold the works of the Lord,
Who has inflicted horrific events on the earth.
He makes wars to cease to the ends of the earth;
He breaks the bow and cuts the spear in two;
He burns the chariots with fire.
"Stop striving and know that I am God..."[5]

Cindy's heart was beginning to shift, and she could feel it.

She took a few more bites of dinner and then set her plate on the couch beside her. She didn't know what was happening, but she wanted to be present for it.

She muted the television and pulled her blanket around her shoulders.

As she closed her eyes, she could hear her parts wondering what was happening. "Let's just wait a minute and see what the Lord wants to do," she said to them softly.

They were all still. She could see them standing in a circle. There was the angry part, the scared part, even the little one, and many others. They were all still. She couldn't remember a time before when that had happened.

We haven't lost any parts, someone said. We are all here.

As the stillness settled her being, she began to notice even more parts within her mind's eye. These self-images had been there all along, but she had never really acknowledged them before. There were a few more children and a couple of adult parts that entered the scene. They all stood together. They stood and were still, together.

A tear ran down Cindy's face. This was the most beautiful sight she had ever seen. It was more than that, though. She could feel the beauty of the moment.

"Lord, I don't know what You are doing here," she began, "but I give You full permission to do it." She raised her hands to shoulder level as an act of surrender to the Lord, letting her blanket fall onto the couch.

The picture in her mind was changing. Angels were coming in to stand with her self-images—just a few. They were singing something:

There is a river whose streams make the city of God happy,
The holy dwelling places of the Most High.
God is in the midst of her; she will not be moved;
God will help her when morning dawns.
The nations made an uproar, the kingdoms tottered;
He raised His voice, the earth quaked.
The Lord of armies is with us;
The God of Jacob is our stronghold.[6]

It was Psalm 46, the passage the pastor had read on Sunday as part of his sermon. He had talked about the kingdom of God and how heaven related to our lives on earth. He had talked about the spiritual battle we face and aligning with the Lord in this battle.

"I want to align with You, God. I want to fight for the kingdom of God. I just don't know how." She waited.

The angels continued to sing. Her parts were now sitting in the middle of the growing circle of angels, just watching and listening as the mighty worshippers of the Most High God sang praises.

As Cindy watched them, she began to pray, "I used to think these parts were my battle. My dissociation ruled my life, and I fought it hard, God. But You showed me they are just me. They aren't my enemy." She thought for a moment. "Then I thought my parents were my battle. Oh, how I longed to be free from their grip!" For a moment, a flash of the mighty, black storm the Lord defeated for her last week went through her mind.

"Oh, thank You, God, for delivering me from that stronghold!" she burst! This time, she could feel the gratitude deep in her heart.

"I know I have more healing to do, but I want to fight, I want to fight for You, God. Show me how! I know that Satan is our enemy, but I don't know how to fight him. I don't even know if I am capable of fighting him."

Cindy felt a deep calling of the Lord come into her spirit. Michael felt it too.

"Show me what this calling is. Give me a strategy, Lord, and I will follow You into battle."

Her parts all nodded in agreement with her statement, some with more enthusiasm than others, but all agreed. She couldn't remember this happening before either.

As soon as she felt the agreement, the atmosphere in the room began to return to normal. The picture in her mind of the angels singing around her parts faded, and the strong presence she had felt was lifting. Cindy knew with all of her being that she was called to do something for God. She just wasn't sure what.

As the Spirit of the Lord lifted, her parts slowly began to process what had just happened.

But we aren't even healed yet. How can we fight some holy battle?

I don't like fighting.

The little one started to whimper, but one of the newly revealed older parts went over and held her.

How do we know what to do?

How will we ever agree on what to do?

"It's okay," Cindy interrupted them. "The Lord will show us. We just have to wait."

Cindy pulled her green blanket over her lap and nestled into the corner of the couch to soak up what was left of her experience.

Michael and his troops were still in full-on worship of the Most High God. Although the cloud had lifted, they honored and praised Him well into the night.

Cindy slept on the couch until about 2 a.m. when she awoke long enough to move to her bed.

At 7 a.m., the alarm on Cindy's phone went off. She was surprisingly alert as she reached for her phone and dismissed the alarm. Without thinking, she climbed out of bed and headed in to make her morning coffee. By 7:30, she was dressed and sitting at the kitchen table with a warm cup of coffee in her hand, looking out the window, hoping to see her favorite bluebird. By 8 a.m., she had finished her coffee and breakfast, with no visit from the bluebird, and was heading for the living room.

Beside her couch, on the tall cherry bookcase, she found her Bible. It had been a while since she had tried to read it. Last time it didn't work so well, but today she just felt like holding the holy book in her hands. She flipped through the pages, not looking for anything in particular. She settled on re-reading Psalm 46[7], the passage she had heard on Sunday, and then again last night in her vision. She began to read:

"Psalm 46, 'God is our refuge and strength, an ever-present help in trouble. Therefore, we will not fear, though the earth gives way and the mountains fall into the heart of the sea, though its waters roar and foam and the mountains quake with their surging. Selah.'"

This passage resonated with the part of her that struggled with fear. She continued, now reading out loud:

"Verse four. 'There is a river whose streams make glad the city of God, the holy place where the Most High dwells. God is within her; she will not fall; God will help her at break of day.'"

Cindy could feel the little one as she read this passage. The older self-image was still holding the image of Cindy as a little girl. Somehow these verses brought her a sense of peace and steadfastness.

"Verse six. 'Nations are in uproar, kingdoms fall; He lifts His voice, the earth melts. The Lord Almighty is with us; the God of Jacob is our fortress. Selah.'"

That is the God I want to serve!

The angry part was feeling drawn into the Lord's battle.

"'Come and see the works of the Lord, the desolations He has brought on the earth. He makes wars cease to the ends of the earth; He breaks the bow and shatters the spear: He burns the shields with fire.' Amen!"

It was Cindy's voice, but she was pretty sure it was the angry part's response to this passage. Something about bringing justice to pass in such a powerful way made this part stand up and take notice.

"Verse ten and eleven says, 'Be still, and know that I am God; I will be exalted among the nations, I will be exalted in the earth. The Lord Almighty is with us; the God of Jacob is our fortress. Selah.'"

Something about that last line brought a sense of strength and passion to Cindy's heart. Her entire being was feeling united in this Psalm. She closed the Bible and sat with her hand resting on the cover.

"Dear Lord, I still don't know what You want from me, but I am Your servant. Please lead me."

She waited for a response from the Lord but heard nothing. After a few more minutes of waiting, she began to get fidgety. She laid the Bible down on the couch and decided to head into town for some shopping. It would still be another few days before she got her first paycheck, so she couldn't really spend much, but she wanted to get out of the house, and she didn't have much else to do.

Forty minutes later, she pulled up to the local strip mall. It was an older mall with only about sixty percent of the stores in use, but it was still good for shopping. She went into the candle store first. She loved the smells in here. The décor was eye-catching, and the salesperson was friendly. There was a coffee cup left on a shelf in the back, and Cindy smiled as she thought of Amanda's illustration at work yesterday. Absentmindedly, she picked up the cup and tossed it in the trash as she left the store.

The next store sold kitchen wares. She didn't really like shopping for the kitchen. She rarely cooked and didn't even know what most of the gadgets were for. Still, something about the store drew her in. After walking around for a few minutes, she realized it was the display in the window. She stood inside gazing at the rainbow bowls and measuring cups stacked in a perfect design. Beautiful! She loved the colors.

About an hour later, she realized that she had been assessing every store she entered with the big-picture perspective that Amanda had taught her the day before. She made mental notes about what worked and didn't work about each store for her as a customer, and then she tried to imagine what the overall strategy was behind the various decisions made by the store owners.

Once she realized what she had been doing, she decided to make a game out of it. She couldn't spend any money, so she might as well find another way to entertain herself while shopping, and entertaining it was!

Some stores were easy to figure. The clothing store for twenty-somethings was playing the latest pop music and had trendy-looking displays of outfits and accessories. It smelled a bit strong, but she guessed it was a popular cologne. The sales reps were all in their twenties, and sporting clothing was sold at the store. It was easy to see the strategy here.

Other stores were more challenging. Three doors down from the young and trendy clothing store was a Christian bookstore. The layout was tight. It was difficult to squeeze through some of the aisles, and there were fragile knick-knacks here and there. Cindy was worried she would knock something off and break it. There was a children's section with toys, books, and a television playing a Christian kid's cartoon at the very back of the store. If she could barely walk in the store, she couldn't imagine bringing a small child all the way through to the back where the toys were.

The only strategy she could imagine the store owner having was trying to get all items out to make the most of the building's space. Still, it didn't seem like a great strategy. She did like the attractive displays and the pleasant aroma of the store, though.

One by one, she examined the stores, their appeal, and the potential strategy behind their design. It made for a fun afternoon, and she thought the experience would certainly help her at her new job.

It had been an easy day for both her and her angelic band. There were a few stores where potential battles lay wait, but the Lord had gone before them and kept the evil at bay. "There seems to be a specific strategy the Lord is using with Cindy right now," one of the angels observed.

"I agree," Michael stated. "I will be curious to see how this unfolds."

After a quick bite to eat, Cindy headed home for the evening.

The evening was uneventful. Cindy headed to bed that night, content but a little disappointed. She had hoped God would speak to her about her new mission. She had a deep passion for fighting alongside the Lord in His battle, but she just didn't know where to begin. She had hoped maybe He would have spoken to her today.

As she laid in bed, she imagined the Lord sending a person with a special word of direction for her. Or maybe He would send an actual angel. That would be fun!

Of course, maybe He needed to integrate all of her parts first so she would be whole and could put up a better fight for the kingdom of God.

That last thought brought with it a pang of discouragement. She had been striving for integration as long as she knew about her dissociation. She thought she was close several times, but she never really was. The more time passed, the less she believed total healing was even possible. If God needed healing to happen so she could fight in His battle, then she may never really be of value to the kingdom.

Her own thoughts frustrated her.

Why would you end such a fun day with such a terrible thought? she chided herself.

After some bantering with her parts, Cindy finally drifted off to sleep.

Wednesday morning, Cindy felt more tired than she should. Somehow, after good days, the few she had, she always felt exhausted.

"Coffee, first," she said as she pulled on her robe and headed into the kitchen. She could hardly stay awake at the table, but somehow, she managed to get everything done and make it to work on time.

"Good morning, Cindy!" Amanda greeted her at the door. "How was your day off?"

"Pretty good, actually." Cindy smiled.

"Wonderful!" Amanda motioned toward the back offices. "Unfortunately, I won't be working with you today as I expected. I had a meeting come up with the central office." She held the glass doors open for Cindy as they walked into a small conference room. "I have some more training videos set up in here for you to watch." She indicated a remote control and a TV hanging on the wall. "Just watch through these three DVDs, and I will come and check on you after lunch."

"No problem," Cindy responded as she mustered a smile. She was looking forward to working with Amanda today, and she definitely felt too tired to watch videos.

Oh, well, she thought. *I guess every day can't be fun.*

Amanda left, and Cindy started the first video.

By lunchtime, Cindy was done with training videos. Well, she wasn't actually done, but she felt done. It was good to get up and stretch her legs for a bit on her lunch break. She walked down the block to a little Mexican restaurant where they served the best hot tortillas. She sipped her iced tea while munching on tacos and taking in the scene around her.

They have no clue.

Who?

All of the people here; they have no clue!

No clue about what?

Who I am. Do you think they would just politely sit about if they knew a crazy lady was sitting here?

Cindy froze. She didn't expect the hostility that came from that last statement. She was simply allowing her parts to express themselves, but that last line took a turn.

Michael saw her body change and was on alert in an instant. "Something is happening," he alerted the others.

Swords were drawn in a flash as Hezek began to scan the area for intruders.

"What do you mean?" Cindy asked herself.

You know what I mean. You are crazy. We are crazy. You shouldn't have a job. You should be in a hospital, drugged up, where you can't hurt anyone.

But, but, Cindy stammered for a reply.

But nothing! You got free from death—whatever that was about—and shame, but, admit it, you will always feel shame to some degree, and now your parents. But are you really any different?

Cindy set her taco down, stunned but listening. Whoever this part was, seemed to have a good point.

You are exhausted all of the time. You lose time. You can't find your keys or your phone most of the time. You still have no idea how to have a decent relationship with anyone. Should I go on?

Cindy was silent.

Soft crying.

Cindy could see in her mind's eye one of the older parts she had met in the last session come and comfort the little one who was crying.

Oh, yes, and there's that, her! What a baby! And you, sitting here in this restaurant, listening to all of these voices in your head—crazy!

"Who is this, who is talking?" Cindy stammered.

There was no reply.

Her hand was shaking, and she could feel tears welling behind her eyes.

"Cindy?"

She didn't respond. This voice was different. Where was it coming from?

"Cindy? It's me, Mrs. Watson."

Startled out of her thoughts, Cindy looked up. She blinked a few times, focusing her eyes on someone nearby.

Mrs. Watson was standing at her table.

"Oh, hi." Cindy could feel her face warm with embarrassment, and her head still felt dizzy.

"I was just walking by, and I saw you sitting here outside eating. It's a beautiful day." Mrs. Watson looked around smiled. She glanced back at Cindy, tilted her head, and asked, "Are you doing okay? You look a little stressed."

Tears began to well up in Cindy's eyes. "I'm okay."

Mrs. Watson opened her mouth as if to say more, then she closed it, politely nodded, and to Cindy's great surprise, sat down at the table.

Cindy blinked away her tears. She followed Mrs. Watson's gaze across the small outdoor eating area toward a few hearty-looking rose bushes that lined the edge of the parking lot.

"Pretty, aren't they?"

Cindy nodded in agreement. Her body began to relax slightly.

"Stay on alert, but I think we might be in the clear," Michael told his troops.

"Thank the Most High God for this interruption!" Gabe declared.

As Mrs. Watson's angelic group joined with Cindy's, they would indeed be prepared if an attack should happen.

"Funny thing, those rose bushes are a beautiful part of God's creation. They smell beautiful, they look beautiful, and roses are a very hardy plant."

"That's true." Cindy was still feeling a little disoriented.

"The thing is, as beautiful as the rose bush is, it is also dangerous."

"The thorns," Cindy responded to no one in particular.

"Yes, the thorns, they can be quite a problem." Mrs. Watson paused and glanced at Cindy just for a moment. "And as hearty as the rose bush is, tiny little bugs can destroy it overnight."

"I didn't know that." Cindy was fully engaged in Mrs. Watson's plant lesson now.

"My aunt had a rose bush, one of the most beautiful ones you have ever seen!" Mrs. Watson had turned now and was holding Cindy's attention with her gentle gaze. "These terrible little weevils moved into her garden and went to work on her rose bush. Within two days, the leaves were torn and fallen, and the enormous rose blooms had been eaten to the stems. My aunt was heartbroken. She loved that bush. She didn't know what else to do, so she dug it up and threw it in the trash."

Cindy could relate to the bush. She felt as if she had been destroyed by some evil bugs and tossed in the trash. A tear ran down her face. She let it fall.

"Well, I saw the bush and decided I wanted to try to make it live again." She smiled. "I planted it at home and did a lot of research on rose bushes."

The waitress interrupted the story to fill Cindy's water glass and bring Mrs. Watson one of her own.

"Anyway," Mrs. Watson started again, "I started by planting the bush in a planter on my small patio. It took weeks of care and pruning and watering before I saw life begin to return to the plant. There were days when I didn't think it was possible. I almost threw it out myself more times than I can count." She laughed a light, airy laugh. "But I persevered."

"Did the plant live?" Cindy couldn't help but ask.

"Why, yes, it did. It didn't get back to its full size with the enormous rose blooms I was used to seeing for a couple of years, but eventually, it did!"

Cindy nodded and took a drink of her tea to try to clear the lump from her throat.

"I think people are a lot like that rose bush." Mrs. Watson looked back and studied the rose bush as she continued, "We can be hurt or even destroyed, but with care and perseverance, the Lord can bring us back. Through His grace, we can receive His love. The love of God is stronger than anything else."

God's grace allows us to receive His love, Cindy thought.

Mrs. Watson paused, then looked back at Cindy. "We each have a purpose, something the Lord wants to pass through us to others. When we find that, we find a reason to persevere."

Cindy didn't know what to say. The story spoke to her deeply, yet, she had no idea what her purpose was. She knew God wanted her to live and flourish just because she was His, but she had no idea what she could possibly contribute to anyone. Especially with her life.

Mrs. Watson took one last drink of water and then stood. "I have to be getting back. I will be out the rest of the day, but I will see you next week."

As Mrs. Watson started to walk off, Cindy stood. "Mrs. Watson?"

"Yes," she replied, turning to face Cindy.

"Thank you." It was all she could say, but somehow Mrs. Watson understood completely.

"You are welcome, Cindy." She squeezed her arm gently and then walked away.

Michael and his troops stood down as it appeared the trouble was over.

Cindy paid her bill and left a tip on the table. After a last drink of tea, she decided to take a closer look at the rose bush. She walked over and examined it closely. She could smell the flowers, quite beautiful, and although the blooms were not as large as the ones on Mrs. Watson's aunt's bush, they were still lovely.

Cindy smiled and turned to walk away. Before she did, she heard a familiar sound. As she turned to look, she saw a bluebird land on one of the branches of the rose bush.

Cindy smiled. "I understand, Lord. I understand."

Chapter 17

Soon, it was Thursday morning. The sun was shining brightly through the little kitchen window over Cindy's favorite breakfast spot. Session was today, and Cindy was certain it would be difficult but equally hopeful the Lord would meet her there.

As she drank her coffee and munched on a bagel, she thought about her week. Work was going well, church was going as well as it had in a long time, and she felt more confident about her future.

How can you be confident? You have no idea what other bomb is going to drop!

"Ah, you are all still here," she said out loud with a smile.

Of course, we are.

I am still scared.

You are a baby!

The little one began to cry again, and Cindy could sense one of the older parts go to her to bring comfort.

Cindy sat her cup down and picked up her fork to pick at her eggs.

See, you don't even know how to help yourself! Today is going to be a wreck like every other session.

Cindy just listened. She didn't push away the harsh dialogue. She didn't try to rationalize or argue. She just listened.

This whole thing is stupid. Nothing is better, and nothing will ever be better.

It was hard not to sink into the depressive thoughts flooding her mind, but Cindy held her ground emotionally. "Walk by faith, not by sight," she whispered to herself.

You have no faith!

Cindy sighed.

"Time to get ready for work," she stood, placed her plate and cup in the sink, and headed for her room to change.

She was halfway to the store when she realized it was Thursday. No work.

Stupid, why can't you even get this right? Sessions are always on Thursday, you were just thinking about session today, and now you are halfway to work before realizing your mistake. Stupid.

"She is starting to wither," Salih observed.

"I know," Michael nodded. "She is so much stronger than she used to be, but the battle is getting harder."

"How can we help her?" Rabok asked.

"Just stay nearby," Michael instructed. "The Holy Spirit will be settling here soon. I received a message last night that today will be a significant session for the glory of the kingdom of God."

All nearby nodded and returned to their posts.

The parking lot was nearly empty when Cindy pulled her little blue Toyota into her usual spot.

In the spiritual, nothing could have been further from true. A battle had already started above and around the little country counseling office.

Cindy smiled as she opened the door and looked up to the sky. The sun was bright. She closed her eyes to feel the warmth on her face.

The spiritual clouds were building like smoke from a forest fire. The angels could see nothing except their charge and the path to the office. Snarls and hisses could be heard from every direction, and the amount of fear in the air was almost palatable.

A smile swept across Cindy's face as she heard a bluebird singing from somewhere. She wasn't sure where, but she knew it was nearby.

As she walked into the office, swords were clanging, putrid puffs of red and black smoke were dissolving right and left, and the quiet hum of the worshipping angels was the backdrop to it all. Surrounding Cindy as she walked were Rabok and Salih, along with a few extra ministering angels that had been sent from the throne of God to join in today's victory.

The Holy Spirit was ministering to her directly in a personal and intimate way. She could sense it, her angelic guard could see it, and the darkness feared it.

"Hi, Cindy," Mary greeted her from the door of her office as Cindy entered the building. "Come on back."

Mary's smile was pleasant and aided the Holy Spirit in His work.

Over the next twenty minutes, the two talked about Cindy's week and her newfound freedom.

"The only thing I don't understand is why do I still battle so hard? Why am I still dissociated? What am I supposed to do now?"

"These are very normal questions, Cindy. You have had several major healings happen over the past few months, and it sounds like your life is so different."

"It is different, in some ways, but it is painfully the same in others." She paused as if making a mental list of the differences. "I have a job now, which is great, but I can still barely make it to work, and some days I don't. I am finally free from my parents, and I am great with that, but I am still lonely and don't know how to have good relationships. I still lose time, forget where I put my keys, and this morning, I was halfway to work before I realized it was Thursday. I don't even know where to focus anymore."

Mary could feel Cindy's frustration. "Let's just take a minute and ask the Holy Spirit to join us."

As Mary and Cindy prayed, light began to stream out from between the ministering angels surrounding Cindy. Before, the Holy Spirit had been contained very near to her; now, He was taking over the room. Demonic entities were appearing all over the room as the light of the Lord illuminated their positions. The warrior angels nearby didn't even need to raise their swords, as the demons instantly fell to the power of the light of God.

Cindy breathed in deeply. "I want the Lord to show me my purpose. I want to fight for Him, but I don't know how."

The words felt so final as they left her mouth. They were from the very depth of her being. It was as if her purpose was to ask about her purpose. The question made her feel complete in a way she wasn't expecting.

"Okay, let's ask," Mary said with a big smile.

"Father God, You heard Cindy's question. What can You show her about her purpose?"

The two were quiet for a moment, waiting on the Lord.

A picture began to take shape in Cindy's mind, and she described it to Mary:

She saw yarn began to extend to earth from heaven. First, it was thin strands woven and crocheted together in a beautiful and delicate pattern, there were half a dozen strands, or so that were growing and moving in a vivid and elegant dance. Then, strands began to pair with other strands creating even more complex and beautiful strands. This continued for a few moments. "DNA. I think this is DNA when it leaves the Lord and comes to earth. Bloodlines marry, babies are conceived, and bloodlines merge creating new and different designs, each beautiful in its uniqueness."

Cindy watched for a few more moments. Soon, the picture began to darken. Strands began to warp. Some looked darker, others looked hard, and others seemed to be covered in slime. There were still a few strands that revealed their delicate origins, but as more and more strands paired with others, the darkness began to spread throughout the bloodlines, increasing with each generation. Cindy opened her eyes with a start. "It's too much. It's too much evil, too much sin."

"It is, Cindy. The earth is covered with evil and sin. Let's ask the Lord about it."

Cindy hesitated and then closed her eyes. She saw Satan with a satisfied, mocking grin on his face as he reviewed his handiwork, polluting the bloodline with sin and corruption. He mockingly looked at the Lord as he gestured toward all he had done. The product of centuries of planning, deceiving, and manipulating humankind. His satisfaction was palatable and disgusting. The Lord did not even acknowledge his presence, though. The Lord had kept His eyes on His children the entire time, continually creating new strands, repairing and strengthening strands that were damaged, and blocking other strands from connecting. If this were a numbers game, God would have easily lost. His holy strands were few and appeared delicate—even fragile—next to the corrupt strands. But it wasn't a numbers game. It had never been.

The Lord suddenly stopped his movements for just a moment. A smile began to cross his focused face. Satan winced slightly, unsure of what was happening. Satan looked back at his strands, moving a few, checking them to make sure they were intact. All looked as he left it. He clearly had the numbers on his side.

"This is not a numbers game." The words echoed from somewhere, and Cindy saw Satan shudder. "This is about love." As the words formed in her mind, the sword of the Lord began to severe the sin from the bloodlines where it was attached. The Holy Spirit was as skilled as a surgeon as He used the sword to remove the evil that was never intended to be a part of God's children. Then the blood of Jesus Christ began to flow down the bloodlines, and in an instant, the hardness and slime were gone from the remaining God-given strands.

Fear and panic were seizing Satan as he watched the culmination of his life's work crumble. There was nothing he could do. He was paralyzed. Frantically, he shouted orders to a few strands that remained separate from those the Lord was cleansing. These strands had made their choice. They had openly rejected the Most High God, and Satan knew they would be his, but they were not enough. If this were a numbers game, he would lose.

"This isn't a numbers game; this is about love." The words were strong and sure.

Satan cringed and grabbed his head. He detested those words, that statement. He hated it with every part of his being. He shook off the terror and looked up in time to see the cleansing water of the Most High God wash away every last bit of grime from the strands He was cleaning. It was too late. There was nothing he could do.

Satan began to squeeze the black, hardened strands still in his command, and anger exploded from his hands. The scene went black.

Cindy blinked a few times as she opened her eyes. Overwhelmed by the scene, but not forgetting one detail of what the Lord had shown her. Mary was finishing the transcription of the scene as Cindy had described it to her.

The spiritual battle in the room had calmed under the power of God, but Michael and his troops still stood ready to fight if needed. "The rest is between Cindy and the Lord," Michael stated in reverence.

Salih and Rabok relaxed and moved away to allow the Lord to complete what He was speaking to Cindy.

"What does it mean?" Cindy asked as she looked up at Mary.

"The Lord is cleansing bloodlines. This has been His war strategy all along."

"I don't understand. Why would God wait to cleanse all of these bloodlines if He could have done it at any time?" Cindy wondered.

"Did you notice the Lord was cleansing bloodlines throughout that whole process? He never stopped," Mary commented.

"That's true. But at first, He was very selective in where and how He cleansed the strands. In the end, He was cleansing as many as were willing—whole groups at a time—and He had severed off most all of the evil from humanity when He was done. Why didn't He do that sooner?"

"Cindy, the Lord is building an army. He is building the kingdom of God. We are the population that will fill heaven one day. The Bible says that we will rule and reign with Him." She paused as Cindy was taking it all in. "The only way humanity could ever rule alongside the Most High God is if we are developed and matured by Him. He was growing us. He is training us. When Satan thought the evil was corrupting humanity, God knew that the battle was actually strengthening humanity. It is in fighting the evil that our weapons are honed, and our skills are developed for serving in the kingdom of God."

The power of the Holy Spirit in the room was so thick now that Zral and Abei were worshipping on their faces before the Lord. The others were bowing on one knee with their swords laid on the ground before them in honor of the final battle the Lord would one day win.

"Is that why the strands looked stronger and even more beautiful once they were cleansed?" Cindy asked.

"Yes," Mary responded. "Of course, Satan wants a kingdom of his own. He cannot create life, so for him to populate his kingdom, he must corrupt the life that God creates. Because he cannot create, and his corruption pales in comparison to God's creation, he spends decades, even centuries, trying to corrupt the bloodlines enough to drown out the voice of the Most High God flowing through the DNA of humanity. You saw it. Some of those strands took decades, generations, to be as corrupt as they were."

"God knew this process was needed both to separate the wheat from the chaff and also to strengthen and mature His people. I believe, when God's kingdom is ready for their people, and when the people are ready for the kingdom, God knew it was time to end the war with Satan. And there is not a thing Satan can do to stop it."

Cindy was beginning to realize that her journey was about much more than her trauma, parents, or even her bloodline. Our journey has been part of God's war strategy all along. She realized God allowed Satan to bring in the corruption to give humanity a choice. Every choice leading to the Lord strengthened her and other believers. God also allowed Satan to think he was succeeding, while all along, God was using the very things that Satan was doing to continue to strengthen every person who wanted to be a part of God's family for the kingdom of God.

She thought about her journey over the last few years in particular. She was certainly stronger now. Her love for the Lord was deeper, and she understood things in ways she never thought possible. God never wanted evil to happen to her, but it did. So, He made sure that it made her stronger and better.

"God takes every single thing that happens to us and uses it to strengthen us," Cindy commented.

"He does," Mary responded.

"I always thought God couldn't use me because of the terrible things that happened to me. I thought I couldn't really have a purpose, at least nothing meaningful." Cindy paused as she thought about what she wanted to say next. "But it turns out; it isn't about my purpose at all."

Mary nodded as Cindy continued.

"It is about God's purpose. It was about His purpose all along." Her thoughts were starting to connect. They were starting to mirror the thoughts of the Lord in ways she didn't know was possible, and she didn't know if she would even be able to remember these thoughts tomorrow, so she wanted to say them all out loud right now while she felt them so deeply. "His purpose is to build the kingdom of God, the one on earth, and the one in heaven. His purpose is to work all things together for our good and the good of His kingdom." She thought a moment. "And one way He does that is by taking what the enemy means for a curse and using it for good."

"You are starting to see the Lord in a different way, aren't you?" Mary asked.

"I am. God is fighting for me. He is fighting for everyone." Cindy reached for another Kleenex to wipe her tears and blow her nose one last time. She wanted to be a part of God's war strategy. She wanted to use all that God had grown and developed in her to fight. And now she knew how.

"Let's let the Lord wrap up our time today," Mary said with a grin. She closed her eyes, and Cindy did the same.

As Cindy's eyes closed, she could see dozens, maybe hundreds of angels dressed in war clothes surround her in layers. They all looked outward with their swords drawn, saluting the Most High God who was sitting on a white horse in the clouds. Michael, Ronan, and the others could see what the Lord was showing Cindy, and they smiled at glory being revealed.

The scene was magnificent and powerful, but there was an air of battle surrounding Cindy. The true battle was just beginning. As she looked around within the circle made by the warring angels, she could see the few dozen parts that had not yet integrated. Each part began to link arm and arm with another, and as they did that, they each received their armor from the Most High God for the battle that would be ahead. When their inner circle was complete, one of the little ones raised her sword and said, "To God be the glory, both now and forevermore!" The others raised their swords and echoed her decree, "To God be the glory, both now and forevermore!"

They didn't know exactly what would be ahead, they didn't even know what tomorrow would look like, but they had a new purpose. They had the heart to see the kingdom of God strengthened. They had a new passion and vision for serving their Lord and Savior. They had a war strategy.

Endnotes

1 Psalm 95:1-6 (NASB)
2 Psalm 69:33-34 (NASB)
3 Psalm 91:1-3 (NIV)
4 Psalm 107:1-3 (NIV)
5 Psalm 46:7-10 (NASB)
6 Psalm 46:4-7 (NASB)
7 Psalm 46:1-11 (NIV)

Coming Soon!

Book Two: *War Strategy*

* * *

For more information and help regarding dissociation, please visit:

TraumaCopingSystem.com.